"You Listen To Me, Jase Calhoun. I Agreed To Run Your Office, Not Your Whole Darn House."

She marched to the stove. "If you think you're going to turn me into your personal servant," she warned as she twisted open a can, "you've got another think coming. I don't need this job. In fact, I still don't know why I agreed to come here."

"Because you love me."

Feeling his breath on her neck, she whirled, unaware that he'd moved. "As a friend," she informed him, and pushed a hand against his chest to keep him from drawing any closer. "Nothing more."

Hiding a smile, he reached to thread a tendril of hair behind her ear. "Are you sure about that?"

Dear Reader,

The excitement is growing as the search for the missing pieces of the deed continues. I don't know about you, but I think I've lost a piece of my heart to each of the heroes in the series—even the soldiers from the Vietnam War who only appeared in the prologues. All of the heroes have displayed characteristics I respect in a man: loyalty, integrity, honesty...well, a few of the guys may have fudged on that last one a bit, but considering the motivation behind their deceptions, I can forgive them.

I hope you enjoy this newest addition to the series. A tall, dark and handsome cowboy and the woman who has secretly loved him since she was a young girl...it's the stuff romance is made of!

Happy reading!

Peggy

THE TEXAN'S SECRET PAST

PEGGY MORELAND

Published by Silhouette Books
America's Publisher of Contemporary Romance

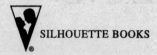

SILHOUETTE BOOKS

ISBN-13: 978-0-373-76814-1
ISBN-10: 0-373-76814-1

THE TEXAN'S SECRET PAST

PEGGY MORELAND

published her first romance with Silhouette Books in 1989 and continues to delight readers with stories set in her home state of Texas. Peggy is a winner of a National Readers' Choice Award, a nominee for *Romantic Times BOOKreviews* Reviewer's Choice Award and a two-time finalist for a prestigious RITA® Award, and her books frequently appear on the *USA TODAY* and Waldenbooks's bestseller lists. When not writing, Peggy can usually be found outside, tending the cattle, goats and other critters on the ranch she shares with her husband. You can write to Peggy at P.O. Box 1099, Florence, TX 76527-1099, or e-mail her at peggy@peggymoreland.com.

To the men and women serving our country in Iraq.
May God be with you and keep you safe.

* * *

To every thing there is a season,
And a time to every purpose under the heaven:
A time to be born, and a time to die;
A time to plant, and a time to pluck up that which is planted;
A time to kill, and a time to heal;
A time to break down, and a time to build up;
A time to weep, and a time to laugh;
A time to mourn, and a time to dance;
A time to cast away stones, and a time to gather stones together;
A time to embrace, and a time to refrain from embracing;
A time to get, and a time to lose;
A time to keep, and a time to cast away;
A time to rend, and a time to sew;
A time to keep silence, and a time to speak;
A time to love, and a time to hate;
A time of war, and a time of peace.

—*Ecclesiastes* 3:1-8

Prologue

Unsure of his welcome, Eddie stood on the sidewalk, and stared at the modest frame home. He should've called first, he told himself. Given her some warning. To show up unannounced on a person's doorstep was rude, disrespectful.

But he hadn't wanted to call. He'd wanted to *see* her, *hold* her, *prove* to himself that the image and memories that had carried him through the remainder of the war were real and not a product of his imagination or the booze he'd consumed the night they'd first met.

He remembered the night well.

He'd been in Saigon, celebrating his first leave of duty since arriving in Vietnam, and teetering toward drunk. After months of living with nothing but death and destruction, he'd welcomed the numbing effects of alcohol, the respite it offered from the cold realities of war he lived with every day.

He and some of his buddies were leaving one bar and on their way to another, when they'd spotted a group of American women on the street. There were four in the group; two journalists and two photographers fresh from college and ready to make their mark on the world. As far as Eddie was concerned, there might as well have been only one. He remembered the long, straight blond hair that had curtained her face and dropped to form a *V* that ended in the middle of her back. The incredible blueness of her eyes. The smile that had reached into his chest and squeezed at a heart he'd thought war had hardened to stone.

Romeo, the most outgoing in the band of partying soldiers, was the one who had approached the women and invited them to join the guys for a drink. After a whispered debate, the women had agreed and had walked with the soldiers to the next bar. Eddie was quick to stake his claim on the blond, and parked himself in the chair next to hers. They'd talked, danced, talked some more. Some time in the wee hours of the morning, they'd taken their conversation outside. They'd walked the streets together, oblivious to all but each other. And when they'd approached the hotel where she was staying, she'd invited him up to her room.

The rest, as they say, was history.

They'd made love. Even then he'd refused to think of what they'd shared as anything as common as sex. What he'd experienced with her was incredible, mind-blowing, life-altering. His leave had lasted two days and he'd spent every second of it with her. Sharing his thoughts and dreams, listening as she shared hers. He'd taken her image with him back to camp, to a war that seemed would never end. Clung to the memories they'd made together, as tightly as Poncho, another one of his buddies, had clung to his rosary when he was scared.

He'd written letters to her. Filled page after page after page with words in an effort to express his feelings for her, confessed his fears of dying, the grief and anger that filled him each time a member of his team was killed or wounded. He'd ended each with the same request.

Please wait for me.

He'd never mailed a single one.

How could he when he wasn't sure he'd make it home? Telling her that he loved her and asking her to wait for him had seemed unfair, considering they'd spent a grand total of two days together. Even if she had shared his feelings, how could he place that kind of burden on her, subject her to the grief, the loss, if he hadn't made it home?

So he'd kept his feelings to himself, and held on to her memory as a means of survival.

He'd made it home all right, but he hadn't jumped on the first bus headed for North Carolina to find her. He'd needed time to adjust to life in the States again, come to terms with all he'd experienced.

He'd had to learn how to walk again.

The doctors who'd cared for him had told him he was lucky. A lot of men had lost their lives in Vietnam. He'd only lost a foot. But there were times he didn't feel so lucky. Most were when he thought about seeing her again.

As a result, close to two years stood between his return from Vietnam and now. During that time, he'd wrestled with the expected doubts. Would she be repulsed by the prosthesis he now wore? Would she consider him less of a man because of his disability? Would she even remember him?

There's only one way to find out, he told himself, and took that first unsteady step up the sidewalk that led to her parents' home. Fearing she might be looking out the window, he squared his shoulders and concentrated on making his gait even to hide his limp. At the door, he punched the doorbell and stepped back to wait, rubbing his damp palms down the sides of his legs.

A feminine voice called from somewhere inside, "I'll get it!" Seconds later the door swung open. The woman who appeared wasn't Barbara, but the likeness was close enough to let him know he was probably looking at her mother.

"Mrs. Jordan?" he asked uncertainly.

She looked at him curiously. "Yes, I'm Mrs. Jordan."

He forced a smile past his uncertainty. "Eddie Davis," he said by way of introduction. "I'm a friend of Barbara's. I'm trying to track her down. By chance, is she here?"

"No, she and her husband live in Washington, D. C."

Eddie heard nothing after "husband." The word hit him like a mortar right square in the chest.

"I can get her address for you, if you like," she offered helpfully.

Shaking his head, he took a step back. "N-no, ma'am. That's not necessary. Just passing through. Sorry to have bothered you."

As he retraced his steps down the sidewalk, he didn't bother to disguise the limp the war had left him with. The prosthesis dragged like a leaden weight at his heart.

One

Divorce was hell on a woman.

Mandy Rogers knew, because she'd experienced it first hand. As far as she was concerned, the entire process was like being fed through a wringer washer, then stripped naked and paraded down a city street for all the world to see.

Which was why she'd chosen to move back to her hometown of San Saba, Texas.

She hadn't been running away, she assured herself as she drove down the country road that led to the Calhouns' ranch. Having the support of family and friends while she adjusted to divorce and life as a single woman again was what had persuaded her to move back to her hometown.

But after a mere two weeks, she wondered if she'd made a mistake in coming home.

Her mother was already driving her crazy. Though Mandy was sure her mother meant well, she treated Mandy as if she was suffering from a terminal disease, rather than recovering from a divorce. And the friends she'd thought she'd reconnect with were gone, having left San Saba after graduation, much as she had, and never returned.

Except for one.

Even as the thought formed, she saw him. Jase Calhoun. Walking from the house toward the barn in the distance, his stride long, his gait slow and lazy. The cowboy hat he wore shielded his face, but she didn't need to see it to remember his features. Roman nose, square jaw, chiseled cheekbones, chocolate-brown eyes, and the sexiest mouth in San Saba County.

She gave the horn a tap to catch his attention. He glanced over his shoulder at the sound, then turned fully, pushing a knuckle against the brim of his cowboy hat. A smile slowly spread across his face as he recognized her, and he started back the way he'd come.

She barely had time to climb from her car, before he was scooping her up into his arms and twirling her around. The greeting was classic Jase and delivered to all women, no matter what their age, but he had a way of making a woman feel special, which is exactly how Mandy felt now…and what she desperately needed.

He plopped her back down to her feet and took a step back to give her a long look up and down. "Damn, Red, how long's it been?"

The nickname was one he'd given her years ago and earned him a frown the same as it had then. "Ten years, and my name is Mandy."

Grinning, he scrubbed his knuckles over the top of her head. "Yeah, but Red suits you better." He slung an arm around her shoulders and turned her toward the house. "What are you doing in town? Home for a visit?"

"No. I moved back."

Sobering, he nodded, as he guided her down to sit on the porch steps. "Yeah. I heard you were getting a divorce."

That he knew about her divorce didn't surprise her. San Saba was a small enough town for everyone to know everyone else's business.

"*Got*, not getting," she corrected. "It was final a couple of weeks ago."

He slanted her a look as he dropped down beside her. "You doing okay?"

She lifted a shoulder. "Some days are better than others." Not wanting to talk about her divorce, she laid a hand on his arm. "I was sorry to hear about your mom, Jase."

Dropping his chin, he nodded. "Yeah. It was tough."

"I would have come home for the funeral…"

He gave her hand a reassuring pat. "No explanation needed. You had your own problems to deal with."

"Still, I'd have liked to have said goodbye to her. She was a special lady."

"She was that, all right, and then some." He slapped his hands against his thigh, obviously not wanting to talk about his loss any more than she wanted to talk about hers. "So? Tell me what you've been up to. Are you living with your mother?"

"She wanted me to, but after living on my own for so long… Well, I thought it best, if I had my own place."

"In town?"

She nodded. "I'm renting Mrs. Brewster's garage apartment."

He reared back to look at her. "That dump? I thought that place was condemned years ago."

"It's not *that* bad," she chided, then flapped a hand. "Anyway, it's only temporary. If I decide to stay, I'll find something else."

"Of course you're staying. Where else would you go?"

"Believe it or not, there's a whole world beyond San Saba, Texas."

"Yeah, but San Saba's home. Folks here to look after you."

"I'm twenty-seven, Jase," she reminded him. "I don't need looking after any longer."

"Twenty-seven?" He blew a low whistle. "Man. Where's the time go? Seems like yesterday you were a snot-nosed kid trailing along behind me and Bubba."

"Bubba's been married for ten years and has three snot-nosed kids of his own."

He swelled his chest and preened. "Yeah, and the youngest he named after me."

She choked a laugh. "Hopefully he won't attempt to live up to the name."

He bumped his shoulders against hers. "Ah, now, I wasn't so bad."

She looked at him in disbelief. "Are you kidding me? Either your memory is impaired or you're suffering a strong case of denial. You and Bubba were holy terrors."

"We knew how to have a good time. Was it our fault folks around here lacked a sense of humor?"

"Definitely denial," she decided, then glanced at her watch and rose. "I'd better go."

He caught her hand. "You just got here. Stay and visit awhile."

Though tempted, she shook her head. "I just stopped by to offer my condolences. I need to get back to town."

"What's so all-fired important in town?"

"The superintendent's office. I need to pick up a teaching application before they close for the day."

He stood, but didn't release her hand. "Sounds like you're planning to stay, if you're applying for a job."

She lifted a shoulder. "I've applied other places. Where I land will depend on who offers me a position first."

He slung an arm around her shoulders and walked with her to her car. "You're not working now?"

. "No. Seems a waste, when I'd have to quit in the fall when school starts."

He opened the car door for her, then hooked an arm over it, while she slid inside. "Red a teacher," he said, shaking his head. "Hard to believe."

"Mandy," she corrected, "and I've been teaching school for four years."

He closed the door, then stooped to brace his arms along the open window and teased her with a smile. "Almost makes me wish I was in school again. Bet I'd make better grades with *you* as my teacher."

She gave him a doubtful look. "Only if you applied yourself more than you did the first time around."

He reached inside and stroked a knuckle over her cheek. "Wouldn't have to. You've always had a soft spot for me."

One thing was for sure, Mandy decided as she made the drive back to town. Jase Calhoun hadn't changed one iota in the last ten years. He'd aged some, as was to be expected, but the years had only enhanced his already rugged good looks. But time certainly hadn't changed his personality. His ego was still the size of Texas, and he was still the biggest flirt in San Saba county.

Did he think she had changed? she found herself wondering, and glanced at her reflection in the rearview mirror. She definitely looked different than she had as a teenager. Her features were essentially the same, though more defined, her eyes still a leaf-green, her hair still red. She wore it a little shorter now and styled it more fashionably than the pony tail she'd swept it up into as a teenager, but it was still the same detested red she'd been born with.

But had *she* changed? she asked herself, then sputtered a laugh and turned her gaze to the road again. Oh, God, she hoped so. Thirteen wasn't a pleasant age for any woman to remember. Even less so when that woman had had a crush on her brother's best friend. She winced, remembering the hundreds of ways she'd made a fool of herself in an attempt to get Jase to notice her.

"Past history," she told herself and forced the embarrassing thoughts from her mind. "You got over your crush on Jase years ago."

But as she turned into an empty parking space in front of the superintendent's office, she remembered the feel of his knuckle on her cheek, the teasing glint in his brown eyes, and a delicious shiver skittered down her spine.

She was over him…wasn't she?

* * *

The next afternoon Jase sat at what he'd always thought of as his mother's desk and clicked the mouse again. When nothing happened, he shot a frown at the silent printer and mentally ticked off the steps he'd taken. He'd loaded the pre-printed checks into the machine, as he'd seen his mother do, opened the bank account on the screen, clicked the "Print Check" option, but for some stupid reason the printer wasn't engaging.

Frustrated, he whacked a hand against the side of the monitor, then sank back in the chair with a frustrated sigh. He hated computers. RAM. Gigabytes. Software. Hardware. The techno lingo alone was enough to give him a headache.

He was going to have to find somebody to take over the office duties, he told himself. He would've already hired someone for the job, except he knew that would mean training that someone, and how could he do that when he didn't understand his mother's system himself?

Heaving another sigh, he raked his fingers through his hair and folded his hands behind his head. If only she'd have agreed to hiring an assistant, as he'd begged her to a thousand times over the last couple of years, he wouldn't be in—

He shot up from the chair, the answer to his problem so obvious he couldn't believe he hadn't thought of it before.

Red!

She had worked for his mother while she was in high school, and was bound to have a pretty good idea how the office was run. She was a smart gal. A teacher, for cripes sake! What she didn't know, she could probably figure out. Hell, Red would be the perfect person to take over his mother's duties!

Relieved to know that his days of butting heads with the computer would soon be coming to an end, he grabbed his cowboy hat and headed for the door.

He didn't doubt for a minute that Red would agree to take on the job. People rarely said no to Jase Calhoun.

Especially women.

Jase parked his truck behind Mandy's car and tilted his head to the side to study the garage. For as long as he could remember, Mrs. Brewster's garage apartment had been known as the "Leaning Tower of Brewster"…and it appeared the widow had done nothing to rectify the problem that had earned the structure its name. The house itself had burned to the ground years ago, and rather than rebuild on the exiting lot, the widow Brewster had opted to build a new house in another section of town. All that remained to mark the spot of her former home was a crumbling chimney and the detached garage with an apartment above it.

Why in the world would Red want to live in such a dump? he asked himself.

With a woeful shake of his head, he climbed down

from his truck and headed for the wooden staircase attached to the side of the building. He jogged to the top, rapped his knuckles against the door, then quickly stepped back to avoid the chips of old paint that rained down onto his boots.

"Just a sec," he heard Red call from inside, then the door opened and she appeared, wearing ragged cut-offs and a tank top.

She blinked up at him in surprise. "Jase. What are you doing here?"

He dragged off his hat and gave her his most charming smile. "Paying my favorite girl a call." He tipped his head toward the apartment. "Aren't you going to invite me in?"

"W-well, yeah," she stammered, and opened the door wider.

He started inside but was stopped short by the wall of moving boxes that blocked his way. "Are you coming or going?"

"More like marking time," she replied, and lifted a shoulder. "Seems a waste to unpack, when I don't know how long I'm going to be here." She motioned for him to follow her. "We can sit in the kitchen. There's more room in there."

Jase trailed her through the narrow path between the stack of boxes, gaining a new sympathy for people who suffered from claustrophobia.

"Can I get you something to drink?" she asked.

He pulled out a chair from the table and twirled

it around to straddle the seat. "Wouldn't turn down a beer, if you have one."

She wrinkled her nose. "Sorry. Iced tea or water is all I have."

"Iced tea will do."

While she poured their drinks, Jase looked around. She'd said the kitchen was roomier, but as far as he could see the only difference between it and the living room was the lack of boxes. If he stretched out a hand in either direction, he'd touch a wall.

"Sugar?" she asked, as she sat a glass in front of him.

He glanced up, then shook his head and picked up the glass. "This is fine."

She sat opposite him and took a sip of tea.

"I guess you're wondering why I'm here," he said.

"Well, yeah. As a matter of fact, I am."

He set his glass on the table. "Yesterday you mentioned that you weren't working."

"Not much point in applying for a job, when I'd have to quit in a couple of months." She looked at him curiously. "Why are you so interested in whether I'm working or not?"

"Because I want to hire you."

She bobbled her glass and quickly set it down to keep from dropping it. "You want to *what?*"

"Hire you." He leaned forward, anxious to share his plan. "I need someone to take Mom's place and you seemed the natural choice."

"Why me?"

"Because you worked for Mom while you were in school."

She choked a laugh. "Jase, that was years ago!"

"True, but I figure you'd have a jump on anyone else, since you've done the work before."

Her smile slowly faded. "I don't know that I want a job," she said hesitantly.

"What else have you got to do with your time?"

Her wounded look let him know that he'd said the wrong thing. He quickly reached across the table and covered her hand with his. "I need you, Red. With Mom gone, there's no one to take care of the office. God knows, I've got more than I can handle taking care of the ranch and minding the pecan orchards and getting the cabins and blinds ready for the hunters. I can't take on the office work, too." He gave her hand a squeeze. "Please, Red? Help me out here. You're the only one I'd trust to take on the job."

"I don't know, Jase," she said uncertainly. "What happens when I'm offered a teaching job for the fall and have to leave? What'll you do then?"

Shooting her a wink, he released her hand. "Now don't you go worrying that pretty little head of yours about the future. Just focus on today." He picked up his glass, drained it, then stood, mission accomplished. "You can start first thing in the morning."

Mandy still wasn't sure how Jase had talked her into agreeing to work for him. She didn't want a job.

She'd purposely given herself the summer to adjust to her divorce and being single again.

Don't you go worrying that pretty little head of yours about the future. Just focus on today.

And isn't that just like Jase, she thought as she made the drive to the Calhoun ranch the next morning. Living in the moment without a worry for the future. That had always been his philosophy.

And what many considered his failing.

Jase never worried about anything. He walked slow, talked slow and lived his life his own way, without a care for time or the opinions and feelings of others. Some said he was lucky his parents were wealthy because, if left up to his own devices, Jase would probably never amount to much. Not that he was lazy, Mandy thought in his defense. He simply didn't *care*. Not about public opinion. Not about the future. He lived in the moment. Plans were something other people made. He strolled through life without any goals or ambitions, other than having a good time.

For the teenaged, infatuated Mandy, that trait had only added to the allure of Jase Calhoun.

But she was older now, she reminded herself as she parked in front of the Calhoun home and climbed out of her car, and wiser. She still loved Jase, but her feelings were no longer romantic in nature. She felt for him what she would any old and dear friend.

As she stepped onto the wide front porch, the

front door opened, making her wonder if Jase had been watching for.

"Mornin'," he said cheerfully.

"Good morning," she replied.

He waved her inside. "Come on back and I'll show you where you'll be working."

As she followed Jase through the house to the office near the rear, she couldn't resist peeking into the rooms they passed as she'd always loved the Calhouns' home. Built from native limestone quarried from Calhoun land, the house was spacious, boasting twelve-foot ceilings and plenty of windows to view the vast acres that surrounded it. The decor wasn't what she would have chosen. The colors were boring and the furnishings added without any thought to design or function.

But Katie Calhoun was never one to spend time on anything as frivolous as decorating. Her only interests were her family and the businesses they owned, and that was where she focused her time and skills.

Jase paused before the door to the office. "I put a pot of coffee on. Want a cup?"

She shook her head. "Thanks, but I had my quota before I left home."

"Quota?" He snorted a laugh. "Why put limits on pleasure?" He tipped his head toward the office. "Make yourself at home, while I grab me a cup."

With a rueful shake of her head, Mandy stepped inside and looked around. Not much had changed in the ten-plus years since she had worked for Mrs.

Calhoun. The L-shaped desk still held center court in the middle of the room. Beneath the windows behind it, stood the long credenza of file drawers, which held the files pertaining to the family's businesses. Built-in bookcases lined the walls on either side of the desk, their shelves crammed with books and framed pictures of the Calhoun family.

Crossing to the desk, she smoothed a hand over the flat screen computer monitor occupying one corner, a vast improvement over the dinosaur Mrs. Calhoun had used during Mandy's previous employment. The remainder of the desk was covered with mail.

Puzzled by the sheer size of the pile, Mandy sat down in the chair and picked up an envelope. Her eyes widened when she saw that the postmark was more than three weeks old.

"Looks like you're settlin' in."

She glanced up to find Jase had returned and was taking a seat on the sofa opposite her. "When was the last time you opened mail?" she asked.

He took a sip of coffee, shrugged. "Can't remember. Awhile, I guess. Since before Mom died."

She dropped the envelope and picked up another, this one with a return address from the State Comptrollers' Office. "Are you telling me you haven't paid any bills since your mother's death?"

"I tried a couple of times." He shot a scowl at the computer. "It's that damn thing's fault. Won't let me print anything."

Mandy dropped her elbows to the desk and her head to her hands. "Oh, Jase," she moaned. "You're lucky you're not in jail."

"It's not like creditors are beating down the door," he said defensively. "The people we do business with know I'm good for whatever I owe."

She lifted her head. "I'm sure they do, but in the meantime they're charging you outrageous finance charges and overdue fees. And what about payroll? Please tell me you've been paying the men who work for you."

"Well, of course I have. I wrote the checks out of my personal account."

"Did you make the proper deductions for social security, withholding tax and insurance?"

He looked at her blankly, which was answer enough.

"Oh, Jase," she moaned. "This is worse than I thought."

"Which is why I hired you," he said and stood. Lifting his cup in a gesture of farewell, he turned for the door. "I'll check in with you later."

Panicking, Mandy shot up from the chair. "Jase, wait!"

He stopped and turned. "What?"

She opened her hands. "I don't know what to do, where to start."

"You did this stuff before when you worked for Mom, didn't you?"

"Well, yeah. But that was years ago."

With a shrug, he turned away again. "Then you're a step ahead of me. I've never done it at all."

Left on her own, Mandy was forced to figure out a way to attack the mess she'd been left with.

Deciding the mail had to be dealt with first, she opened it all, and sorted it into piles marked Reply Needed, Bills, Hunting Reservations, Bank Statements. Once that task was completed, she played around on the computer, familiarizing herself with the system and the different software packages Mrs. Calhoun had used. She felt a bit like a burglar or, at the very least, a major snoop, digging through the Calhouns' correspondence and financial records. But she had little choice. In order to understand Mrs. Calhoun's bookkeeping system and her method of conducting business, she had to examine what had been done in the past.

Once she felt comfortable using the computer, she began reconciling the bank accounts. There were quite a few, as each of the family's businesses had its own individual accounts. Among the mail she'd sorted were several statements for Jase's personal bank account, but she set those aside, assuming he'd want to take care of them himself.

By noon, she'd reconciled the accounts for Calhoun Cattle Company, but hadn't even started on Calhoun Pecan Orchards or Triple C Hunting, which was the account set up for the income and expenses relating to the hunting rights they leased each year, as well as the cabins they rented to the hunters.

And her head ached from trying to keep it all straight in her mind.

She couldn't believe Jase had simply ignored the office work, following his mother's death. If it had been anyone other than the Calhouns, she was sure creditors would have filed charges and he'd have wound up in jail. The amount owed in bills alone was enough to make her head spin. She couldn't imagine having that much money, much less *owing* it to someone. But the Calhoun operation was a large one, and a business of that size naturally would generate large expenses.

Hearing footsteps in the hallway, she looked up, just as Jase entered the office.

"I'm starving," he said without preamble.

She glanced at her watch and rose, surprised to see that it was well past lunchtime. "I've been so busy I haven't even thought about food."

He slung an arm around her shoulders and headed her toward the kitchen. "Think about it now. I'm hungrier than a bear."

She tipped her head back to look up at him. "I'm supposed to cook for you?"

He shot her a wink. "Mom always did and you're taking over her jobs."

Rolling her eyes, she headed for the refrigerator.

"I suppose she did your laundry and cleaned up after you, too."

"Laundry, yes. Cleaning, no. When my cabin needs a good shaking down, I'm the one who does the shaking."

She straightened to peer at him over the refrigerator door. "You don't live here in the house?"

He pulled out a chair from the table and sat down. "Not since I was nineteen. I live in one of the hunting cabins."

"Oh." She resumed her search of the refrigerator. "So when are you planning on moving back in?"

"I'm not."

She popped up to look at him again. "You're not?"

"Why should I?"

"The obvious. Because it's here and it's yours."

He shook his head. "I like where I am just fine. There's no reason for me to move."

She glanced toward the door that led to hallway, thinking of the spacious and beautiful house left empty. With a rueful shake of her head, she closed the refrigerator door. "Everything in there is either molded or out of date. You really should have the housekeeper throw it all out, before it starts stinking up the whole house."

"I let the housekeeper go after Mom passed away."

"Why?" she asked, then held up a hand. "Never mind. Then *you* need to throw it all out."

He gave her a pointed look.

Her jaw dropped. "You expect *me* to clean out your refrigerator?"

"You took over Mom's job. She was in charge of the kitchen, as well as the office."

She planted her hands on her hips. "You listen to me, Jase Calhoun. I agreed to run your office, not your whole darn house."

"Then leave it in there," he said. "You're the one who'll have to put up with the stench, not me."

Flattening her lips, she spun for the pantry and yanked open the door. She snatched out two cans of soup and marched to the stove. "If you think you're going to turn me into your personal slave," she warned as she twisted open the cans, "you've got another think coming. I don't need this job. In fact, I still don't know why I agreed to come here."

"Because you love me."

Feeling his breath on her neck, she whirled, unaware that he'd moved. "As a friend," she informed him, and pushed a hand against his chest to keep him from drawing any closer. "Nothing more."

Hiding a smile, he reached to thread a tendril of hair behind her ear. "Are you sure about that?"

Two

"I heard you're working for Jase."

Inwardly groaning, Mandy continued to fold towels. She'd known her mother would eventually find out about her new job, but she'd thought it would take longer than twenty-four hours.

"As a matter of fact, I am," she replied.

"Do you think that's wise?"

The disapproval in her mother's voice was obvious, but Mandy ignored it, hoping to avoid an argument. "I'd go crazy just sitting around the apartment all summer. Working will help pass the time."

"If you'd wanted a job, you should have told me.

I'm sure I could have arranged something for you with one of my friends."

"Arranging" was her mother's term for running Mandy's life, a pastime she'd excelled at, until Mandy had gone away to college.

"I'm sure you could have," she said patiently. "But to be honest, I wasn't looking for a job. Jase offered, and I accepted."

"The two of you alone in that house all day." Her mother clucked her tongue. "It just doesn't look right, Mandy. Not right at all."

The implication was clear, as well as insulting, and had Mandy spinning to face her mother. "For your information, he isn't in the house all day. He's out on the ranch working. I only see him when he comes in for lunch or if he needs something from the office."

"It isn't appropriate," her mother maintained. "And with you being newly divorced, and all…"

"What does my being divorced have to do with anything?" Mandy cried.

"Oh, come on, Mandy," her mother chided. "Surely you must realize everyone will think you've crawled straight from your husband's bed into Case's."

"That may be what *you* think, Mother," Mandy returned furiously, "but I doubt everyone else in town shares your low opinion of me."

"Now, Mandy," her mother soothed. "I'm just trying to help you see what a mistake you're making. How your actions might be misconstrued."

"By whom? You're the only person I know who would even consider such a thing." Knowing she should leave before she said something she would regret, Mandy picked up her laundry basket and headed for the door.

"Where are you going?" her mother called after her.

"Not to see Jase, if that's what you're worried about."

Mandy carried her anger home with her and to the office the next day. She understood now why her brother had packed up his family and moved to Montana years ago. Living in the same town with their mother was proving to be a little too close for comfort.

She'd known her mother wouldn't approve of her working for Jase, which is exactly why she had avoided telling her about her new job. Alice Rhodes had never liked Jase and made no attempt to hide her feelings. It all went back to when Jase and Bubba were in high school. They were constantly getting into trouble, and Alice had blamed Jase for each and every one of their escapades. Bubba was as guilty as Jase, and would be the first to admit it, but Alice had refused to believe her son was anything but perfect.

Mandy considered it a shame her mother didn't feel the same way about her daughter.

"Who put a burr under your saddle?"

Seated behind the desk, she glanced up from the computer screen to find Jase standing in the doorway.

Realizing she was scowling, she scrubbed a hand over the creases in her brow. "Nobody. Just concentrating."

He crossed to stand behind her and peered over her shoulder at the monitor. "Is that the Cattle Company account you're working on?"

Stiff from sitting so long, she stretched her arms above her head, then dropped to her lap with a sigh. "Yeah. I've just about got it up-to-date." Remembering the statements for Jase's personal accounts, she picked up the unopened envelopes from the corner of the desk and handed them to him.

"What's this?" he asked.

"Statements for your personal accounts. I figured you'd want to reconcile them yourself."

He tossed the statements onto the desk. "Wouldn't know how to begin. You do it."

"Are you sure?" she asked uncertainly.

"I've got nothing to hide."

With a shrug, she pushed the envelopes back to the corner of her desk. "I'll take care of them after I've finished paying the Cattle Company's bills."

"Speaking of the Cattle Company. I'm going to take some bulls to the sale tomorrow. They're registered, so I'll need the papers."

Mandy hooked a thumb over her shoulder at the credenza that held the file drawers. "They're probably in there."

"I don't need them right now. Just by morning."

She rolled her eyes. In other words, *she* was the one

who would do the searching, not Jase. "I'll leave them on the desk for you when I leave this afternoon."

He shot her a wink. "That's my girl."

"Your slave, you mean," she grumbled, as he headed for the door.

In the hallway, he stopped and lifted his nose to sniff the air. "Do I smell something cooking?"

"Red beans and rice. I made it last night. Thought it would save me having to stop work to make lunch."

"I don't suppose there's cornbread to go with those beans?" he asked hopefully.

"Yes, and apple pie for dessert."

He clapped a hand over his heart. "Oh, man, I think I'm in love."

In spite of her aggravation with him, Mandy couldn't help laughing at his dramatic pose. "Get out of here, so I can get some work done."

He touched a finger to the brim of his hat. "Yes, ma'am. But you can bet I'll be back in plenty of time for lunch."

Still smiling, she turned her attention to the Cattle Company's bank account again. With the bills she'd sorted for the Cattle Company stacked beside the monitor, she began reconciling the accounts payable and printing out checks, starting with the oldest due and working her way down to the most recent.

An hour later, she stopped and rubbed her burning eyes. Deciding she needed a break from computer work for a while, she scooted her chair around to face the credenza and began searching for the papers Jase had requested for the registered bulls.

Though her previous duties while in Mrs. Calhoun's employ had included filing, she couldn't remember which drawers held what records, which meant she was going to have to do some digging. Resigned to the task, she pulled open the drawer nearest her and quickly thumbed through the labeled tabs in search of the Cattle Company's livestock records.

Not finding what she needed in that drawer, she moved on to the next. When she didn't find the file there, either, she wheeled her chair to the opposite end of the credenza and pulled open the drawer.

"Real Estate Deeds," she murmured, reading the tabs aloud as she thumbed through them, "Vehicle Registration, Vehicle Titles, Adoption Records—" She stopped short and flipped back a file to stare at the neatly labeled tab. *Adoption Records?* Wow. She'd forgotten Jase was adopted. Curious to see what the file held, she started to pull it out, but stopped and bit her lip. That would be snooping, wouldn't it?

What's the harm? He told you he had nothing to hide.

Freed from guilt by her conscience, she slipped the file from the drawer and swiveled her chair around to open it on top of the desk. She quickly thumbed through the documents, most of which were of a legal nature and worded in jargon that only a lawyer would understand. Reaching the last page, she started to close the file, but noticed an envelope clipped to the back of the folder. Handwritten across the envelope's front were the words: For Jase—to be read after my death.

She carefully lifted the edge of the envelope to examine its back and saw that the flap was still sealed. She turned to replace the file in the drawer, but stopped again. By Jase's own admission, he knew nothing about how the office was run or where anything was kept. If she put the file back without showing it to him, it might be years before he found it on his own, if ever.

She tossed the file to the corner of the desk, telling herself she would give it to him when he came in for lunch. Of course, in doing so she would be confessing to snooping, but she'd deal with his wrath, if necessary.

Though she'd placed the file on the desk behind her, she found herself stealing glances at it, wondering what the envelope contained. Not much, judging by it's weight. Probably nothing more than a letter. But why would Jase's mother leave him a letter to find after her death, rather than tell him whatever she wanted to tell him before she died?

Doesn't matter, she told herself, and swiveled her chair to face the credenza again and began searching through the drawers for the papers on the bulls.

Whatever message the envelope contained was no business of hers.

* * *

After setting the table, Mandy shot an impatient glance at the kitchen clock. If curiosity killed the cat, she was currently sitting on death row.

She lifted the corner of the file she'd placed beside his plate to make sure the envelope was still inside, then shut it with a groan without looking. Like it was going anywhere, she chided herself and forced herself away from the table and to the stove to check on the beans she'd put on to warm.

She'd circled the spoon twice around the pan when the back door opened and Jase stepped inside.

"Mmm-mmm," he hummed appreciatively as he tossed his cowboy hat on the counter. "If those beans taste as good as they smell, I'll kiss the cook."

Another time Mandy would've melted at the promise of a kiss from Jase, but at the moment, all she could think about was the envelope his mother had left him, and waved him toward the sink. "Wash your hands while I fill our bowls. There's something I need to show you."

He made quick work of the hand washing and settled himself at the table, his gaze settling on the file, as he dragged his napkin to his lap. "Did you find the bulls' papers?" he asked, as he flipped open the file.

She sat a bowl in front of him, then seated herself at his side. "Not yet. That's the legal papers regarding your adoption."

"Oh." He let the cover drop and picked up his spoon, dipped it into his bowl. "What's it doing in here?"

Fearing she would scream if he didn't open the envelope soon, she gestured to the folder. "I ran across it while I was looking for the livestock records. There's something in the back you need to see."

He shoveled a spoonful of beans into his mouth, then closed his eyes and moaned, while he chewed. "Yep. I'm definitely gonna have to kiss the cook."

"Jase!" she cried in frustration, then flipped open the file herself and removed the envelope. "Here," she said, and thrust it at him. "Your mother left this for you."

He cut a glance at the front of the envelope, then scooped up another spoonful of beans. "What is it?"

"How would I know?" she said, and thrust it at him again.

Frowning, he dropped his spoon into the bowl and took the envelope from her. He slid a thumb beneath the flap, tearing it open, then pulled out the enclosed papers. With a slowness that threatened to drive her crazy, he unfolded the pages and began to read. She watched his face, trying to gauge his emotions, but his expression never once wavered. After reading the first page, he lifted it to look briefly at the second, before folding the papers again.

"Well?" Mandy asked expectantly. "What does it say?"

He tossed the papers onto the table between them. "See for yourself."

She quickly snatched them up and saw that the first page was a letter from his mother.

Dear Jase,

If you're reading this, that means I'm gone. I know it was selfish of me not to share this with you earlier but, to be honest, I was afraid to.

When we first brought you home with us as an infant, your dad and I discussed how we planned to handle the circumstances of your birth and we decided that we would never attempt to hide from you the fact that you were adopted. We also agreed that we'd answer any questions you had about your birth parents, even help you locate them, if you ever expressed a desire to do so. Oddly enough, you never once asked.

I know this won't reflect very well on me, but I was secretly pleased you showed no interest in learning the identity of your birth parents. From the day we brought you home, I considered you my son, and I never wanted to have to compete with anyone for your affection, not even your biological parents.

I know how selfish you must think me, but what's done is done and, if given the chance to do it over, I would do the same. The one thing I can do for you now is provide you with the information you need to locate your birth parents. What you do with it is entirely up to you.

I've enclosed your birth certificate. You'll see that it contains both your mother's and father's names, as well as the city and state in which you were born. That's all I know about your parents, but it should be enough for you to track them down.

I've also enclosed a letter that was given to me when we picked you up at the hospital. It was written by your birth mother and meant for you. I have few regrets in my life, but keeping this from you tops my list. Hopefully you won't hold it against me that I didn't give it to you before now.

If you do decide to try to find your parents and are successful in locating them, please tell them thank you for me. You were the joy of my life, truly a gift from God.

Love,
Mom

"Oh, Jase." Sniffing, Mandy picked up her napkin to dab the tears from her eyes. "That has to be the sweetest thing I've ever read."

He spread butter on a slice of cornbread and

popped it into his mouth. "Mom was a sweet lady," he said, around it, as he chewed.

She stared at him in disbelief. "How can you be so…so *indifferent?* Did you read what she wrote? The part where she said you were the joy of her life, a gift from God?"

"Yeah. I read it."

"And…" she prompted.

Wiping his mouth, he shrugged. "So she loved me. That was no big secret. I loved her, too."

Unable to believe he had read what she'd read and wasn't brought to tears as she was, she set the letter aside and picked up the second document, the birth certificate, to scan. Her eyes shot wide and she reached to clamp a hand over his arm. "Jase, did you see this?"

"What?"

"You were a twin!" She tore her gaze from the birth certificate to look at him. "You have a sister!"

"I'm an only child."

"No," she argued, and scanned the document again until she found the reference to twins. "It says right here," she said, pointing at the box that contained the information. "Your mother gave birth to a set of twins, a male and a female."

"My mother is Katie Calhoun, and she had one son. Me."

Surprised by the anger in Jase's voice, Mandy glanced up and saw that his face was hard as stone.

Silently cursing her insensitivity, she reached out to lay a hand on his arm. "I'm sorry. I didn't mean any disrespect toward your mother. I know you loved her. It's just that this is so unbelievable. Imagine, at your age, finding out that you have a twin? It's like something you hear about on the news!"

When he said nothing in reply, only continued to eat, she slowly withdrew her hand. She glanced at the birth certificate she still held, then set it aside to look at the third page, the letter Mrs. Calhoun had said was written by his birth mother.

To my son,

I'm a writer by trade, yet I can't seem to find the words to express what's in my heart, to share with you the things I want you to know.

Above all else, please know that giving you up is the hardest thing I've ever done in my life. From the moment I felt the first butterfly wings of movement in my womb, I loved you with all my heart.

I'm an unwed mother, but please don't think badly of me or your father. Ours was not a sordid affair. I met your father in Vietnam. He was an American soldier on a three-day leave of duty, and I was a zealous reporter, determined to bring the story of the war home to the American people. I know it sounds ridiculous, but the moment I saw him, I knew I had met my soul mate, the man I would marry and spend the rest of my life with.

Unfortunately, a future for us was not meant to be.

After his leave ended, we went our separate ways, planning to reconnect in the States after he finished his tour of duty. It wasn't until I returned home that I discovered I was pregnant. He was still in Vietnam. I attempted to contact him through the battalion he was assigned to, but was told he was killed while on a mission. To say that I was shocked would be an understatement. The love of my life was gone, lost to me forever. It took days for the reality of my situation to set in. I was alone and pregnant with twins.

Your father and I only spent three days together, yet I felt as if I'd known him all my life. My hope is for you to know him, too. His name was Eddie Davis and he was from Texas. Like everything from his home state, he seemed bigger than life. Tall and lean, he walked slow and talked slow and had the most engaging Texas drawl. He was also one of the most intelligent men I've ever met, as well as the most loving, and he displayed a sense of loyalty few men possess.

You were conceived in love, and it's that

love I lean on for the strength and courage to do what I know needs to be done. I would never be able to provide you with the life you deserve. If yours had been a single birth, things might have turned out differently. But twins? The chance of failing, of being unable to adequately provide for two children is one I simply couldn't take.

One of my nurses suggested that I keep one baby and give up the other for adoption, but how can a mother make such a choice? I certainly couldn't. Not and be able to live with myself. So I'm doing what I feel is best for you. Though it grieves me to do so, I'm placing you into the arms of a couple better suited to fulfill your needs, in a home where you'll have both a mother and a father to care for and love you.

When your father and I said what proved to be our last goodbye, he gave me something to keep for him. It's just a piece of paper, but it's all I have that was his. I've torn it in half, giving you one piece and your sister the other. I hope you'll cherish it as I have.

I will never forget you, son of my heart. You will remain in my thoughts and prayers forever.

Mandy dropped the letter and buried her face in her hands, too moved for a moment to speak.

"Oh, Jase," she murmured, and blindly pushed the letter towards him. "You've got to read this."

She heard the scrape of a chair and snapped up her head to find Jase preparing to leave.

"Thanks for lunch," he said, as he snugged his hat over his head.

For a moment, she was too stunned to speak. "B-but the letter," she finally managed to say. "Aren't you going to read it?"

"Save me some pie," he said, and walked out the door.

Save him some pie?

She stared at the door he'd closed behind him, then looked down at the letter and slowly drew it back in front of her again. Why would he refuse to read the letter his birth mother had written him? Didn't he want to know who his parents were? Why he was given up for adoption?

She shifted her gaze to the birth certificate. And he had a twin. Growing up an only child, she'd think he'd be at least a little curious about his sister. Maybe even want to locate her. Mandy sure as heck would, and she had a brother and already knew what a pain a sibling could be.

And why was Jase so angry?

She picked up the letter his birth mother had written and scanned it again. Coming to the part where his birth mother had mentioned the paper that had belonged to his father, she turned the page over, thinking maybe she'd taped it to the back. Not finding it there, she picked up the envelope and gave it a shake. A torn piece of paper fluttered down and settled on the table.

Holding her breath, Mandy carefully picked it up. She found handwritten words on one side, but the fragment was too small for her to make any sense of the words written there. She turned it over to examine the back and saw the name "Eddie" scrawled there. Remembering that Jase's birth father's name was Eddie Davis, she flipped the piece to the front again to compare the handwriting, and decided the signature on the back was written by a different hand, probably by Eddie Davis himself.

"Wow," she murmured, awed by the realization that she held in her hand the single, remaining link connecting Jase's birth mother and father.

It was mind-boggling, humbling, heartbreaking.

She glanced up at the back door.

And Jase wouldn't even acknowledge its existence, much less cherish it, as his mother once had.

Three

Mandy did her best to put the letters out of her mind, yet they, as well as the birth certificate, haunted her thoughts throughout the remainder of the day.

And no wonder. Finding the envelope alone was enough to send her mind whirling. Add in the emotions and secrets revealed within the letters, and she could think of little else!

She found it hard to believe Jase had never once asked about his birth parents. Yet, according to Mrs. Calhoun, he hadn't. Mandy would've thought any adopted child would be curious to know where he had come from or why his parents had put him up for adoption. She'd read stories in newspapers and magazines about adopted children tracking down one or both of their birth parents, even watched the drama unfold on television right before her very eyes. So why had Case never wanted to find his birth parents?

In retrospect, she could understand why he'd reacted the way he had. He loved his parents and would naturally feel a certain loyalty toward them. But wanting to learn about his birth parents in no way took away from what he felt for his adoptive parents. Not in Mandy's estimation, at least.

"Not your business," she told herself again, and plopped the papers for the bulls in the center of the desk for Jase to find.

After gathering up the outgoing mail, she took one last look around to make sure that she'd put everything away, then headed out.

The odor that greeted her in the hallway was subtle, yet strong enough to remind her she hadn't dealt with the out-dated food she'd discovered in the refrigerator the day before. Knowing that tomorrow it would only smell worse, with a groan, she made a U-turn and trudged her way to the kitchen. After dropping the mail on the center island, she snagged Mrs. Calhoun's apron from its hook on the back of the pantry door and set to work.

With a waste basket propped at her feet, she began pulling items from the refrigerator and dropping them into the basket. By the time she finished, all that remained inside the refrigerator were a jar of mayonnaise and a couple of jars of pickles.

And a very unpleasant smell.

Wrinkling her nose in distaste, she picked up the waste basket and hauled it to the back porch, then returned and filled the sink with warm, sudsy water. Dipping a sponge in the water, she crossed back to the refrigerator and began scrubbing the shelves and walls, working from top to the bottom.

"Well, if it isn't Miss Suzy Homemaker."

She whipped her head around to find Jase standing in the hall doorway, a shoulder braced against the jamb, watching her. Frowning, she yanked open the vegetable bin and scrubbed hard at the wilted leaves of lettuce stuck to the bottom. "Cut the wisecracks or I'll leave it for you to finish."

"Looks to me like you're done." Pushing away from the jamb, he crossed to peer over her shoulder. "What did you do with all the food?"

She turned, sweeping strands of hair from her brow with the back of her hand. "On the back porch. And *you* can haul it to the garbage cans out back," she informed him. "My good nature only goes so far."

Grinning, he bussed her a quick kiss on the cheek and turned away. "Bet you'd deal with the garbage, too, if I asked sweet enough."

Mandy touched a hand to her cheek, momentarily

distracted by the kiss, then dropped it to fist at her side when what he'd said registered. "Don't push your luck," she warned. "I could quit, you know. It's not like I need this job."

He shot her a glance over his shoulder, as he pulled a glass from the cupboard. "So you said." He filled the glass with water from the tap, then turned, bracing his hips against the edge of the counter. "Yet you're here." Hiding a smile, he took a sip of water. "Wonder why?"

Rolling her eyes, she crossed to the sink and reached around him to toss the sponge into the water. "Don't let your ego fool you into believing I'm here for any reason other than friendship."

He caught her arm before she could turn away. "There was a time when you thought of me as more than a friend."

She sputtered a laugh. "I was a teenager with a schoolgirl crush. Believe me, I got over my infatuation with you long ago."

He lifted a brow. "Are you sure about that?"

"Positive. Now, if you don't mind," she said and pulled free. "I need to get this mail to the post office."

She hadn't taken more than a step before he was spinning her back around.

Off-balanced, she planted her hands against his chest to stop her forward movement. "Jase! What are you—"

He covered her mouth with his, smothering her

words, while folding his arms around her and dragging her close. She tried to wrestle free. She really did. For a second. Maybe two. Then he did something with his tongue—a quick flick, a sweep—and she forgot all about fighting and melted against him, winding her arms around his neck and parting her lips beneath his.

She remembered his kiss from a night long ago. His taste. The texture and pressure of his lips. How could she forget something so extraordinary, so wished for? The bone-melting sensual pleasure she had experienced then was exactly what she experienced now. It was if the ten year gap that stretched between the two events miraculously closed, blending them into one moment that hung suspended in time.

The hands that viced her to him were strong and sure, his chest a muscled wall crushed against her breasts that made them ache for his mouth, his tongue. As she shifted to ease the ache, he slid his hands down her back to cup her buttocks, and she rose to her toes, thrilling at the pressure of his groin rocking against hers. He held her there a long moment, his hands molding her buttocks, while he explored the secret crevices of her mouth with his tongue, then slowly withdrew to look down at her.

"You've grown up, Red."

His voice was husky, his eyes a dark, smoky brown.

"M-Mandy," she said, then swallowed hard, to steady her voice, her pulse.

His smile soft, he stroked a hand over her hair, then drew his palm to her cheek. "Yeah, but Red suits you." He dropped his gaze to her lips and swept the ball of his thumb over the lower one. "I just have one question," he said, then looked up at her from beneath his brow. "Do you kiss all your friends like that?"

For a moment, she was too stunned to speak. Thankfully she recovered quickly and flipped the question right back to him.

"Do *you?*"

That night when Mandy climbed into bed she was still wearing a smug smile. Only two words, but her comeback had rendered Jase totally speechless, a major coup for a recently divorced woman, whose self-image had tanked the day she'd found the note her ex had left her informing her he wanted a divorce.

She was so proud of herself! She'd actually flirted with a man, something she hadn't done in years. She'd even actively participated in an extremely sensual kiss.

Not that the kiss had meant anything, she was quick to remind herself. It was nothing more than a ruse Jase had used to get her to admit she considered him more than a friend.

But she had to admit, he'd had her there for a minute. In one smooth move, he'd taken her from insulted female to a puddle of wanton need. Man, that guy could kiss!

Granted, he'd kissed her before, but those had been more like brotherly pecks on the cheek. Only one ranked anywhere close to this one—the kiss they'd shared the night of Bubba's bachelor party.

It went without saying that Mandy hadn't been invited to the party, but that hadn't stopped her from going. At the time, she'd thought herself madly in love with Jase and had crashed the party, just to be near him. Bubba had thrown a fit when he'd caught her, and Jase, always the peacemaker in disagreements between her and her brother, had quickly escorted her from the bar. It was while they were in the parking lot that he'd kissed her.

Both saddened and tantalized by the memory, Mandy pulled the covers to her chin and closed her eyes.

And dreamed of Jase.

As Mandy climbed from her car at the Calhouns' the next morning, thunder rumbled in the far distance. She glanced up and saw a bank of dark clouds building in the western portion of the sky and prayed it wasn't a premonition of approaching doom. She might have gone to bed proud that she'd succeeded in getting the last word, but she'd awakened worrying that she might have jeopardized her friendship with Jase with her sassy comeback. Not that she'd take it back, she told herself. After all, he was the one who'd started it.

Still, she didn't want to chance harming their relationship. There were pitifully few people near her age in San Saba, as it was. She couldn't afford to alienate even one.

Besides, she'd enjoyed verbally sparring with Jase and hoped to again. She couldn't remember feeling so invigorated, so alive, since before her divorce. Of course, a lot of that might be due to the toe-tingling kiss he'd given her, but, hey, a girl took her thrills where she could!

Amused by her thoughts, she skipped up the steps, but found the front door locked. Assuming Jase hadn't arrived at the house yet, she used the key he had given her and stepped inside.

"Jase?" she called, just to be sure he hadn't entered through the back door.

Not receiving an answer, she continued down the hall to the office. She deposited her purse on top of the credenza and saw that the file she'd left for Jase on the desk containing the bulls' papers was missing. Figuring he'd already left to take the bulls to the sale, she sat down behind the desk and turned on the computer. While she waited for it to boot up, she flipped the page on the desk calendar to the current day, then pulled the stack of unreconciled bank statements to the right of the monitor, ready to resume her work on the Calhouns' many bank accounts.

She heard the back door open and frowned. "Jase?" she called uncertainly.

"Yeah. It's me," came his reply.

Seconds later he stuck his head inside the office. "I'm heading out to the sale. Back later this afternoon."

"Watch the weather," she warned. "A storm's brewing."

"Ten-four." He turned away, then stuck his head inside again. "Oh. And to answer your question... only the female kind."

Mandy stared a moment in confusion, then burst out laughing.

Score one for Jase.

"Hey, Calhoun."

Jase glanced up and grinned as his buddy Mark Shillings dropped down on the bench beside him.

"Hope you came to spend some money," Jase said, and tipped his head toward the show ring where the auctioneer's staff worked to keep the livestock moving. "I've got some bulls up today."

Mark shook his head. "Don't count on me running the bid up. I'm here to buy heifers." He glanced around at the crowded bleachers. "You oughta do okay, though. Doesn't look like the weather scared off any buyers."

"Damn good thing," Jase replied. "I'd hate to think I hauled my bulls all the way here for peanuts."

The two focused on the ring where the auctioneer's staff was herding in a new lot of cattle to auction off.

"Heard you hired Bubba's sister to work for you," Mark said after a moment.

Jase hid a smile, remembering the sound of Red's

laughter when he'd left that morning. "Yeah. Had to hire somebody. I've pretty much let the office work go since Mom passed away."

"Is she doing a good job?"

Jase shrugged, his attention caught by an exceptionally good looking heifer in the ring. "All right, I guess. She worked for Mom while she was in high school, so she knows the ropes."

Mark poked an elbow against Jase's ribs. "Bet that's not the only reason you hired her."

Jase glanced his way. "What's that supposed to mean?"

"She's a divorcée," Mark said, as if stating the obvious, then waggled his brows. "And you know what they say about divorcées."

"What's that?"

"They're hot to trot."

"Jeez, Mark," Jase said in disgust. "We're talking about Red here, Bubba's kid sister."

"So? I've seen her around town since she moved back and she sure as hell doesn't look like anybody's kid sister to me." He gave Jase's ribs another poke. "Wouldn't mind going a round or two in the hay with that sweet little thing myself."

In the blink of an eye, Jase had Mark by the front of his shirt. "You keep your hands off, Red," he growled. "You hear me?"

Mark lifted his hands. "Sure, buddy. Sure. Whatever you say."

Jase glared at him another second, then dropped his hand.

Eyeing Jase warily, Mark smoothed a hand over the front of his shirt. "You coulda just told me you'd already staked a claim," he grumbled.

Turning his scowl on the show ring below, Jase said again, "She's Bubba's sister."

Mandy pressed her nose to the window, trying to see the driveway. But it was impossible. The rain was coming down so hard, she couldn't see two feet beyond the front porch.

The storm had built all morning, turning the sky into a caldron of black swirling clouds, but it hadn't started raining until noon. The wind had picked up shortly thereafter, stripping leaves from the trees and battering the house like a demon trying to get inside. Fearing a power outage, Mandy had shut down the computer, but had continued to work in the office, sure that the storm would blow over soon.

When it hadn't abated by six o'clock, she'd begun to think she was going to be stuck at the Calhouns' all night. The dry creeks that crisscrossed the country roads that led to town were known to flood during a normal rainstorm, and this storm was anything but normal.

But it wasn't the thought of being stuck at the Calhouns overnight that had her currently pacing the living room. It was the fact that Jase wasn't home yet.

When he'd left for the livestock sale, he hadn't mentioned what time he planned to return, but she had thought he would be back by now. The sales rarely lasted past two o'clock. Three at the latest. The sale barn was a little over an hour's drive, which meant, even if he'd stayed to watch the sale to it's end, he should've returned hours ago.

Knowing how dangerous it was to drive in weather like this only added to her concern. Visibility would be marginal, due to the heavy rain. And the empty cattle trailer Jase was pulling would be the same as pulling a kite. She could well imagine what kind of havoc the wind was playing with it, whipping it from one side of the road to the other. A good gust of wind could flip the trailer and take the truck with it.

The image was nightmarish enough to have her running to the phone and punching in the number to his cell. After only one ring, his voice mail clicked on. Stifling a moan, she hung up the phone and wrung her hands.

"He's okay," she said out loud, willing it to be true. "He probably stopped somewhere to wait out the storm."

To keep her mind off her worries, she decided to prepare a meal, in the event he was hungry when he made it home. She was standing in the pantry surveying what grocery items were on hand, when the lights blinked out.

Thrown into pitch-black darkness, she grabbed for the doorjamb, momentarily robbed of her sense of balance. She gave herself a moment to adjust to the darkness, then slowly made her way across the kitchen to the sink. Once there, she rifled through drawer after drawer, in search of a flashlight or emergency candles. Finding a flashlight in the last drawer, she flipped on the switch. A faint beam of light flickered briefly, then blinked out.

Swearing under her breath, she tossed the useless tool back into the drawer. Now what? she asked herself in frustration. Without electricity, she couldn't cook, watch television or listen to the radio.

There was nothing left for her to do but wait.

Resigned to her fate, she groped her way through the darkness to the living room to resume her watch. Overhead the rain pounded the tin roof, but beneath the deafening sound came the low rumble of a diesel engine. Praying it was Jase, she hurried to the front door and swung it open. Rain, driven beneath the covered porch by the wind, pelted her face. Holding an arm up to protect her eyes, she looked out and spotted a dim set of headlights through the dark haze and rain. Though she knew it had to be Jase returning home, she didn't release the breath she was holding until she saw him jump down from the cab of the truck and make a dash for the house.

"Damn!" he swore, as he leaped over the steps

and onto the porch. "It's coming a real frog-strangler out there."

She was so relieved to see him, she had to fight the urge to throw her arms around him and simply hold him. To keep herself from doing so, she hugged her arms around her waist. "It started around noon and hasn't let up since. Are the roads flooded?"

He peeled his poncho over his head and tossed it to the porch before stepping inside and closing the door behind him. "A few. All of them will be if this keeps up much longer." He dragged off his hat and slapped it against his leg, sending rain droplets flying, as he looked around. "Is the electricity off?"

"For about fifteen minutes now. I looked for a flashlight, but the only one I found had a dead battery."

He started toward the rear of the house. "Mom keeps candles in the pantry."

Mandy followed close on his heels, using his footsteps as a beacon to guide her through the darkness. In the kitchen, she waited by the island while he dug around inside the pantry.

Within moments, candlelight flickered from the candles he lined up on the island's surface, giving the kitchen a soft, warm glow.

He glanced her way, as he lit the last one. "Better?"

She released a long breath and smiled. "Much. I forget how we depend on electricity until I'm without it. No television. No radio. No stove." She shrugged. "I guess I'm spoiled."

"Aren't we all," he replied and drew the match before his mouth to blow it out.

The sight of his puckered lips jerked Mandy's mind to the kiss they'd shared, making her remember how his lips had felt on hers. The texture, the pressure, the indescribable flavor, the heat. Feeling the flutter of arousal in her stomach, she forced herself to look away. "I'd offer you something to eat, but there isn't anything that doesn't require cooking."

"I bet we can scrounge something up." He ducked back into the pantry and came out holding a large can of chili. "We'll heat it up in the fireplace in the den. It's a little warm inside for a fire, but if it gets too hot, we can always open a window."

Mandy rubbed her hands up and down her folded arms. "To be honest, a fire sounds good. I got wet and I never left the porch. I imagine you're soaked to the bone."

He looked down his front. "Only from the knees down. The poncho kept the rest of me dry." Tipping his head toward the cupboards, he said, "Grab a couple of bowls and some silverware. We'll set up camp in the den."

"All right."

After gathering the requested items, she picked up a candle from the island and made her way to the den, where Jase was already busy building a fire in the fireplace. She set the bowls on the hearth out of his way, then scooted back to sit on the sofa to watch.

She'd always considered Jase a virile male, but he had never appeared more so than now. Crouched as he was, the muscles of his thighs and calves strained against the legs of his damp jeans, while those on his back rippled and bunched each time he stretched out an arm to add a log to the fire. She released a long breath, fully aware the heat warming her cheeks was due to more than the fire.

He pushed his hands against his thighs and stood. "We'll let it burn down a little, before we heat up the chili."

"Okay."

He crossed to the sofa and dropped down beside her with a weary sigh. "Man, what a day."

"Did you get the bulls to the sale?"

"Yeah." He hooked the heel of one boot over the toe of the other and pushed it off, then started on the other. "Got a good price, too," he said, as he stretched out his legs. "I suppose that makes having to swim all the way home worth it."

She gave him a doubtful look. "You really didn't have to swim, did you?"

Chuckling, he shook his head. "No. Though I probably could've made it here faster, if I had."

She shivered, remembering the horrible catastrophes she'd imagined. "I was so worried."

He glanced her way. "Why?"

She rolled her eyes. "I think that would be obvious, what with the storm, and all. And you were so late getting home. You should have been here hours ago."

"If you were worried, you should've called."

"I did. It went straight to your voice mail."

He lifted a shoulder. "In weather like this, I'm surprised you were able to get through at all."

After the stress-filled day she'd spent worrying about him, she found his cavalier attitude more than a little irritating. "It would have been nice if you'd called *me*."

"Why would I do that?"

"Are you saying it never occurred to you that I might be worried?"

"No, as a matter of fact, it didn't."

She tossed up her hands. "That is *so* like you. Not giving a thought to anyone but yourself, while here I was pacing the house for hours, imagining all kinds of awful things."

"What kinds of things?"

She ticked items off on her fingers. "Like the trailer jackknifing. The truck being swept off a bridge by high water. Like *you* drowning." Realizing her temper was rising right along with her voice, she dropped her hands to fist in her lap.

"You're really upset, aren't you?"

She spun on the sofa to face him. "You're darn

right I am! I've been worried sick not knowing where you were, if you were safe, and wondering if I should call the highway patrol or the hospital to find out if you were alive."

Hiding a smile, he caught her hand and tugged her back to sit beside him again. "Next time I'll call."

She folded her arms across her chest. "You darn well better."

He leaned close, bumping his nose against her cheek. "Forgive me?"

Jutting her chin, she turned her face away. "No. I'm mad."

"What'll it take to get you un-mad? A tickle?" He ran his fingers up and down her ribs.

Determined to hang on to her anger, she caught her lower lip between her teeth, refusing to smile.

He scooted closer, so close she could feel his breath on her neck. "Or maybe a kiss," he suggested.

Four

Jase had never considered Red as anything more than a kid sister and had treated her as such, which was why he'd all but jumped down Mark's throat at the auction when his friend had made that lewd comment about wanting to go a round or two in the hay with Red. Big brothers looked out after their little sisters and that's exactly what he considered Red, his kid sister.

Or he had up until that very un-sister-like kiss the day before in the kitchen. But that kiss had taught him a few things.

Namely that Red wasn't a kid any more.

That kiss had relieved him some, too, as it had

proved to him that the attraction he'd sensed building inside him since the day Red had shown up unannounced at the ranch wasn't a figment of his imagination or, worse, the result of him spending too many nights alone. Bubba's kid sister had definitely grown up.

If any doubts had lingered, Red dispelled them when she whipped her head around to face him, at his suggestion of a kiss as a way to get her un-mad. He'd bet the profit he'd made on his bulls that her intent was to tell him he could take his suggestion and put it where the sun don't shine. And she *was* saying something.

Whatever it was, it was lost on him.

All he saw was one-hundred percent pure woman. He didn't know what it was about the combination of fiery green eyes and a mane of red hair that turned him on, but it delivered a kick stronger than a mule's.

While her lips were still moving—probably with words meant to singe his hide—he cupped her face and brought her mouth to his. He felt the shock that shot through her, swallowed whatever words remained on her tongue, and settled in to seduce her.

He knew immediately it wasn't going to be easy. She shoved a hand against his chest, as if to push him away, but he countered the move by closing his fingers around hers and drawing her hand up to drape around his neck.

He tasted the rain on her lips—or maybe it was

from his—and something else. Coffee? He didn't waste any time deciphering the flavors. He was too busy working her blouse up her back so he could get to bare skin.

To his surprise, she didn't go postal on him when flesh met flesh, as he'd expected. Instead, she melted against him like an ice cube left out in the sun. He felt the swells of her breasts slowly flatten against his chest, the languid curl of her fingers in his hair.

"You're not playing fair," she murmured against his mouth.

Hiding a smile, he nibbled at her lips, while lightly trailing a finger up her spine to the bra strap that stretched across her back. "How's that?"

"I wasn't through being mad at you."

He flicked a finger over the hook. "Does that mean you've forgiven me?"

She drew in a sharp breath as the clasp came free, and released it with a breathy, "Maybe."

He drew a hand around to her front and cupped a breast. "How about now?" he asked and raked a thumb over the nipple.

Her only response was a low moan.

Chuckling, he shifted her onto his lap. "I'll take that as a yes."

The change of position gave him better access to her breasts and he was quick to take advantage of the situation. With his mouth on hers, he slipped his hands beneath the front of her blouse and molded his fingers over her breasts' fullness, measuring the shape and feel of them. Each stroke of his fingers drew a new moan from her that vibrated against his lips and tightened his groin. Catching a nipple between two fingers, he teased it into a tight bud, then went to work on the other one.

He soon realized that touching wasn't going to be enough. He wanted to see her. Withdrawing his hand from beneath her blouse, he began freeing the buttons.

He'd unfastened two when her hand closed over his. "Jase, no. We shouldn't."

Her protest was weak, at best, and with a little persuasion, he was sure he could change that no to a yes.

Shifting his hand over hers, he pushed it down to hold against his arousal. "Feel that?" he whispered, and nipped at her mouth. "That's what you do to me. You make me hard. Make me want inside you."

He felt the tremble in her fingers, the slow curl of them around his sex, and knew he was a heartbeat away from that "yes."

Warming her lips with his breath, he caught the lower one between his teeth and gave it a gentle tug of encouragement.

With a shuddery sigh of surrender, she began to move her fingers down his length. Up, down. Up, down. Increasing the pressure with each stroke, giving him a sense of the need building inside her, while doing a damn good job of fanning the flames of his own. He felt the surge of blood that hardened

his sex and thrust his tongue between her parted lips
to tease her with what was to come.

Finding the buttons of her blouse again, he freed
the remainder, then used the flat of his hands to push
the blouse, as well as her bra straps, to her elbows.
Anxious to see the treasure he'd uncovered, he tore
his mouth from hers to stare. Flush with passion, her
breasts rose and fell with each ragged breath she drew.

"Damn, Red," he murmured, awed by her beauty.
He reached out to close a hand over a breast and the
nipple he'd teased into turgidity nudged the center
of his palm.

Unable to resist, he dipped his head and opened his
mouth over the nipple and circled it with his tongue.

Gasping, she grabbed his head and held him to
her. "Jase."

He heard the urgency in her voice, as well as the
need, and lifted his head to kiss her again. "In my
wallet," he mumbled against her mouth, as he
stripped her blouse away and started on her slacks.
"Protection."

He felt her fumbling at his back and hooked his
arms around her and stood, giving her access to his
back pocket and the wallet tucked inside. While she
searched for the condom, he debated the comfort of the
sofa over that of the rug spread in front of the fireplace,
and sank to his knees, deciding the rug offered more
room.

He lowered her down, then stood, his gaze on her,

as he stripped off his clothes. That she was aroused was without question. Passion stained her skin a rosy pink, glazed her eyes. Yet he saw the flicker of uncertainty in them as she offered him the condom. Knowing it was up to him to put her at ease, he quickly ripped off the packaging and unrolled it over his sex.

Kneeling to straddle her, he braced a hand on the rug at either side of her head, then leaned down to brush his lips across hers. "Comfy?"

She gulped, nodded. "You?"

He shifted, gathering her hips more tightly between his knees, and smiled. "Gettin' that way."

Whatever uncertainty she'd experienced was gone now. Her lips were hot beneath his, her tongue demanding as it met and danced with his. He tasted her need, felt its urgency in the hands she clasped against his back, dragging him closer. Heard it in the soft whimpers that vibrated against his mouth. Answering that need, he slipped a hand between them and cupped her mound. She arched high at his touch, her mouth opening beneath his in a silent cry of pleasure. Finding her already moist, he slid a finger inside and she buried her face in the curve of his neck to smother a moan.

"Jase, please," she begged.

"Spread your legs," he said breathlessly, and quickly sank his hips into the V she created for him. With his sex poised at her center, he drew in a last bracing breath, set his jaw and pushed inside.

Her nails dug into his back, but he felt no pain. Every nerve in his body was focused on the exquisite pleasure of being completely wrapped in her warmth.

"Come with me, Red," he whispered against her ear, and pushed his hips against hers.

She moved with him, matching him stroke for stroke, her hips pumping in rhythm with his. Heat surrounded him, pressed at him, seemed to strip the room of air. Ignoring it, he pressed on, blinded to everything but the glove-like grip her walls had on his sex, the soft slap of flesh meeting flesh as their hips met.

He felt her stiffen, her body straining as if toward an unreachable goal, and knew she was close. Folding his arms around her head, he closed his mouth over hers and thrust one last time, burying himself deep inside her.

She arched high and hard, her legs convulsing against his. Stripped of what self control he'd managed to hold on to, he pushed deeper and found his own shuddering release.

With his chest heaving like bellows, he collapsed against her and buried his face in the curve of her neck. He heard the wood shift on the grate, the ticking of the grandfather clock on the mantle and knew he hadn't died and gone to heaven. Gathering his strength, he lifted his head to look down at her…and was sure he'd never seen a more beautiful sight. Her eyes were closed, her lips—swollen from his kisses—curved in what he could only describe as a rapturous smile.

Humbled by her expression, he stroked a thumb beneath her eye. "You okay, Red?" he asked softly.

A sound rose from her throat that was half purr, half hum. "Yeah," she said, releasing it on a sigh. "You?"

Grinning, he dropped his mouth to cover hers. "Workin' on it."

Upon awakening the next morning and finding herself snuggled against Jase's chest, Mandy was immediately struck by two thoughts.

And regret was definitely not one of them.

The first was that all the dreams she'd woven as a teenager of making love with Jase Calhoun had been a colossal waste of time, as they fell pitifully short of the real thing. The man had more moves than a U-Haul and the endurance of a marathon runner, something she'd failed to factor into her dreams, due to her immaturity.

The second was that her mother was right…she had crawled straight from her husband's bed and into Jase's.

The first thought drew a satisfied smile.

The second set her teeth on edge.

Technically she supposed her mother was right, since Jase *was* the first man she'd slept with since her divorce. It was the "climbing straight from" part she had a problem with, as she felt it was inaccurate and totally unjustified. She and her husband were separated for over eight months before their divorce was final and hadn't been intimate for several months prior to that, which meant nine months stood between then and now.

But Mandy knew it wasn't the lapse of time that concerned her mother.

It was the man she had chosen to sleep with.

Troubled by the thought, she glanced at Jase, who slept opposite her, and reached to comb back the hair from his forehead. She'd always attributed her mother's dislike for Jase, to the scrapes he and Bubba had gotten into together as teenagers. But she wondered now if there was more to it than that. There were other boys in the group Bubba had run around with, and her mother had never treated any of them with the disdain she had Jase. Besides, that all happened years ago. If nothing else, surely time would've softened her feelings toward him.

"Does my hair look bad or something?"

Unaware that Jase had awakened, she dragged herself from her thoughts and focused on his face. "Well, no," she said in confusion. "Why?"

"You were frowning at it."

Smiling, she drew her hand to his cheek. "There's nothing wrong with your hair. In fact, you look adorable."

"Adorable?" Grimacing, he scrubbed his knuckles over his head, making his hair stick up every which way. "Chubby-cheek babies and fat-bellied puppies are adorable, not men."

"I suppose you'd prefer I'd said drop-dead handsome."

He dropped an arm over her waist and dragged her hips to his. "Now you're talking."

Laughing, she pushed a hand against his chest. "You're ego is positively scary."

"Can I help it if I know my strengths?"

"Make that terrifying," she amended.

Hiding a smile, he tucked his face into the curve of her neck. "Storm's over."

She glanced back at the window. Though moisture still clung to the glass, it was no longer raining and the wind had died down, leaving an eerie silence behind.

"Do you think the roads are clear?" she asked uncertainly.

"Doesn't matter if they are. You're not going anywhere."

She whipped her face around to peer at him. "Well, of course I am. I have to shower and change clothes."

"You can shower here." He lifted the sheet and peeked beneath it. "And I kinda like what you're wearing now."

Laughing, she pushed at his head. "You would," she said, and rolled from the bed.

He lunged to grab her, but she quickly side-stepped. "Uh-uh-uh," she said, wagging a finger before his face. "I've got to go home and get ready for work."

"All right," he grumbled, "but I'm driving you." When she opened her mouth to argue, he held up a hand. "Think about it. If the roads are still flooded, my truck is higher off the ground than your car."

Knowing he was right, she began picking up her clothes. "Okay. But step on it. It's already past eight."

The drive to town proved to be a testament to the brutality of the previous day's storm. Full grown trees, uprooted by the high winds, blocked portions of the highway, while foot-high water rushed across the bridges, pushed there by rain-swollen creeks.

But the biggest shock came when Jase pulled his truck into Mrs. Bertram's driveway.

"Oh, my God," Mandy whispered staring at the collapsed building.

"It's a wonder it stood as long as it has," Jase said grimly.

"But my things!" Mandy cried. "Everything I own was inside that apartment."

"Hope you had renters' insurance."

He watched the blood drain from her face, which was answer enough for him. Sliding the gearshift into reverse, he started to back from the drive.

She clamped a hand over his arm. "Where are you going?"

"I'm taking you back to the ranch."

"But my things," she said, helplessly.

He tipped his head toward the collapsed building. "I'm not letting you go crawling around in that pile of rubble. It's too dangerous. I'll drop you off at the ranch, grab a couple of the men and come back and dig out what I can."

She shook her head. "No. This is my problem. I'll handle it."

"But it isn't safe," he argued, then heaved a sigh, knowing by the stubborn set of her jaw he was wasting his time.

Jase might have gone along with Mandy's refusal to let him bring along any of his men, but he wasn't about to let her tackle the job alone. After loading a trailer with what equipment he thought he'd need, he drove her back to town himself.

While she stood by and watched, he used the forklift he'd brought along for the job to remove debris layer by layer, exposing what lay beneath. The work was slow and tedious, but care was needed to prevent further damage to what possessions remained.

From his elevated position on the forklift, it appeared everything in the kitchen was pretty much lost. Shards of broken dishes and glass were scattered everywhere, and chunks of splintered wood were all that was left of her table and chairs. The den hadn't faired much better. Her sofa was crumpled beneath a fallen beam, and the boxes she's stored in the room were either crushed by the roof when it caved in or soaked with rain.

After removing what debris he could with the forklift, he parked the machine, then walked back to help Mandy inspect the boxes he'd managed to remove. As he watched her pick through them, he silently cursed himself for not insisting she stay at the ranch. He couldn't imagine what thoughts were going through her mind, but the tears sliding sound-lessly down her cheeks told him the loss cut deep.

Unable to watch her suffer any longer, he crossed to pull her into his arms.

She curled her fingers into his shirt and buried her face against his chest.

"Everything," she sobbed. "I've lost everything."

"Not everything," he reminded her. "You're here, aren't you? If you'd been at home—" He squeezed his arms more tightly around her, knowing damn good and well she wouldn't be standing here with him now, if she'd been in the apartment when the storm had hit.

Sniffing, she pushed back from his arms. "I know. And you're right. I should be thankful I'm alive." She glanced toward what remained of her apartment, and fresh tears welled in her eyes. "But what am I going to do? Where will I live?"

"The ranch, that's where."

She snapped her gaze to his. "At the ranch?"

Although he'd made the offer without thinking,

now that he thought about it the ranch seemed the perfect solution. "Why not? You need a place to stay and the house is empty. And just think of the gas you'll save," he said, hoping to tease a smile from her. "No more driving to work. You'll already be there."

What items they managed to salvage from the debris barely covered the bed of Jase's truck. Mandy was sure, if they'd searched longer, they would've found more, but she felt she'd taken enough of Jase's time as it was, and had insisted upon return-ing to the ranch, knowing he had his own storm damage to deal with.

After hauling her sodden boxes of clothing to the laundry room, he'd left to inspect his pecan orchards to see how his trees had weathered the storm.

Mandy had showered and changed into a pair of sweats Jase had loaned her, then returned to the laundry room to see what clothing could be saved. She'd filled the washer with the first load, when the door bell rang. Holding a hand against the towel wrapped turban-style around her wet hair, she hurried to the front of the house.

Her eyes shot wide when she opened the door and found her mother standing on the stoop.

"Mother! What are you doing here?"

"Looking for my daughter, that's what," her mother snapped.

"I'm so sorry," Mandy said guiltily and ushered her inside. "I should have called. I've been so busy dealing with everything, I didn't even think—"

Her mother snatched her arm free. "You rarely do, which is why I'm constantly having to save you from yourself."

Stung by her mother's remark, Mandy could only stare.

"Since you appear unharmed," her mother went on, "I take it you weren't at home."

"N-no," Mandy stammered, finally finding her voice. "The road to town was flooded, so I stayed here last night."

Pursing her mouth in displeasure, her mother plucked at the sleeve of the sweatshirt Mandy wore. "I suppose that belongs to Jase."

"Yes. He loaned it to me. I ruined the only clothes I had with me when we were digging my things from the debris."

Her mother dropped her hand. "Oh, Mandy," she said wearily. "Will you never learn?"

"Learn what?" Mandy asked in confusion.

"That Jase Calhoun is nothing but trouble."

"Mother!" she cried. "Would you stop? Jase is *not* the evil person you make him out to be."

"He's a womanizer."

"He's a *flirt*," Mandy returned. "There's a difference."

"He's a womanizer. His only interest in you, or

any woman for that matter, is what you can do for him in bed."

"That's not true. Jase…is my friend."

Though Mandy hesitated only slightly in defining her relationship with Jase, her mother picked up on it immediately and narrowed her eyes in suspicion. "You've slept with him, haven't you?"

Mandy opened her mouth to deny the accusation, then closed it, refusing to lie.

Her mother humphed. "That's what I thought." She waved an impatient hand. "Get your things. I'm taking you home before you make a complete fool of yourself."

"No."

Her mother's brows shot up. "What did you say?"

"I said no," Mandy replied, then walked to the door and opened it. "I'm not going anywhere, but *you* are."

"You're asking me to leave?" her mother asked incredulously.

"No, I'm *telling* you."

Her mother jerked up her chin and marched to the door. "Don't come running home to me when he's through with you," she said, as she stalked by Mandy. "You've made your bed, now lie in it."

Mandy gave the door an angry shove, slamming it behind her mother, then sank to the floor in a heap, dropping her head to her drawn up knees. Why does she have to ruin everything? she asked herself miserably. Why can't she just live her life and let me live mine?

No answer was forthcoming, but Mandy hadn't really expected one. She'd been asking the same question most of her life and had yet to come up with a plausible explanation.

"Are you staging a sit-in?"

Mandy lifted her head to find Jase approaching from the rear of the house and sent up a silent prayer of thanks that her mother had left before he returned.

Grimacing, she pushed to her feet. "Something like that."

"What's with the Carmen Miranda getup?"

She blinked in confusion. "What?"

He gestured to the towel wrapped around her head. "Add some fruit and you could pass for her twin."

With a rueful smile, she dragged the towel from her head and scrubbed a hand over her still-damp hair. "I haven't had time to dry my hair." Recalling the cause for the delay, she scowled. "I had company."

"Who?"

"My mother."

He blew a silent whistle, as if narrowly escaping a brush with disaster. "Can't say I'm sorry I wasn't here to say hello."

Mandy tossed up her hands. "What is it with you two?"

"With me, nothing. With her...." He lifted a shoulder.

"If you're referring to the trouble you and Bubba got into, all that happened years ago."

"Some people have a hard time letting go of the past."

She hesitated a moment, unsure if she should tell him the purpose of her mother's visit, then decided he had a right to know. "She doesn't approve of me staying here."

He dropped his chin, nodded. "Can't say I'm surprised." He waited a beat, then looked up at her from beneath his brows. "Does that mean you're going to find someplace else to stay?"

She searched his face, wondering if he regretted making the offer, but found nothing in his expression to suggest he'd changed his mind. "If it's all right with you, I'd prefer to stay here."

He lifted a shoulder. "Your choice."

He started to turn away, but she caught his arm. "Jase, wait."

He glanced back. "What?"

Unsure how to say what was on her mind, she laced her fingers together and twisted them nervously. "I just wanted to…well, to say I'm sorry."

"You have nothing to apologize for."

She flattened her lips. "No, but my mother has plenty."

Chuckling, he slipped his arms around her waist. "Don't let it bother you, Red. It doesn't me."

She dropped her forehead to his chest. "How can you be so forgiving, when she's so mean to you?"

"You know what they say. 'Sticks and stones may break my bones—'"

"'—but words will never harm me,'" she finished for him, then lifted her head to smile up at him. "I really am sorry."

He gave her butt a reassuring pat. "Forget it. I have."

Mandy lined up on the vanity what toiletries she'd managed to unearth from the debris and tried hard not to think about all she'd lost. To be honest, she wasn't even sure what all she *had* lost. There were still a few boxes she needed to go through, and she was sure more of her things would surface during her next search through the wreckage.

But some things she knew were lost to her forever.

She gave herself a shake, refusing to let her mind go there. She was alive and she had a place to live. That was what she would focus on. The positive.

But she'd no sooner dispensed with one negative thought, when another surfaced.

Her mother.

She sank to the side of the tub with a groan, knowing she'd angered her mother by refusing to leave with her. But her mother had made her mad, too, she thought defensively. Saying all those ugly things about Jase and treating Mandy as if she were a recalcitrant child. It was just so humiliating. So *wrong*.

Forget it. I have.

"Easy for you to say, she muttered, remembering Jase's advice. "She isn't your mother."

Heaving a sigh, she pushed to her feet. She'd give her mother a couple of days to cool off, then she'd go and talk to her, try to make her see that Jase wasn't the awful person she accused him of being.

"Hey, Red! Where are you?"

Hearing Jase's shout from another part of the house, she hurried from the bathroom. "In here," she called, and all but bumped into him as she dashed out into the hallway.

"You through unpacking?" he asked.

"If you can call it that, yes."

He hooked an arm around her neck and pulled her along with him. "Good. I thought we'd go for a ride. Check on the cattle."

She stopped short, dragging him to a stop, as well. "Ride, as on horseback?"

"Well, yeah. Can't very well drive through the pastures after all the rain we've had. We'd get stuck for sure."

"I don't know, Jase," she said hesitantly. "I haven't ridden a horse in forever."

He snorted a laugh. "Hell, Mandy. It's like riding a bike. You never forget how."

When she remained doubtful, he gave her a tug

to start her down the hall again. "Don't worry," he assured her. "Once you're in the saddle, you'll remember how it's done."

Remembering how it was done wasn't what bothered Mandy.

It was the soreness she knew would follow that worried her.

After two hours in the saddle, she knew she'd been right to worry. The muscles in her thighs were screaming in agony and she'd lost all feeling in her butt. And they still had to make the ride back to the barn. Promising herself a long, hot bath when they returned to the house, she squeezed her legs against the mare's sides, urging the horse into a trot, in order to catch up with Jase.

"I haven't seen any breaks in the fencing," she said as she drew up alongside him.

"Looks like we lucked out," he agreed. "Lots of limbs down, though, and a couple of trees uprooted. The men will have their hands full for a while cutting and hauling wood." He tipped his head toward a group of trees. "Let's check on the cabins."

He clicked his tongue and sent his horse into a lope. Stifling a groan, Mandy did the same.

By the time she caught up with him again, he was swinging down from the saddle. "Gonna check for leaks," he said and passed her his reins. "Won't take but a minute."

Mandy shifted in her saddle, trying to find a more comfortable position, while she watched him push open the door to the first cabin and disappear inside. When he reappeared seconds later, he called to her, "This one held," and headed for the second.

Gathering his horse's reins more firmly in her hand, she urged her own horse forward, hoping to save Jase some steps. She stopped her horse before the second cabin just as he jumped down from the porch.

"Any leaks?" she asked, as he took the reins from her.

Shaking his head, he swung up into the saddle. "None visible." He shot her a glance. "How're you holding up?"

She gave him a thumbs up sign.

"If it's okay with you, I'd like to stop by my cabin and clean up."

She shrugged. "Fine with me."

He tipped his head again, indicating an opening through the trees. "We'll take the shortcut through the woods."

Mandy, nodded. "I'm right behind you."

Once beneath the canopy of trees, the light changed dramatically. Tree limbs crisscrossed overhead, blocking the late afternoon sun and casting long shadows along the path. The soggy leaves that covered the faint trail softened the rhythmic clip-clop of the horses' hooves, adding to the solitude.

Riding single file behind Jase proved to be the distraction Mandy needed to get her mind off her aches and pain, as the rearview of Jase was almost as good as looking at him from the front. He rode with the reins gripped in one hand, his boots braced against the stirrups, his butt lifted slightly from the saddle. Legs toned from years of riding hugged the horse's side, making her remember what those legs had felt like pressed against hers.

Fearing she would soon be drooling if forced to ride behind him much longer, she was relieved when the trees gave way to a clearing. Nestled in its center stood a cabin. Built from logs and native stone, his cabin appeared larger than the other two they had checked.

Drawing to a stop in front, Jase swung down from his saddle and tethered his horse to the porch railing. Mandy's dismount was slower and definitely more painful. As soon as her feet touched the ground, her knees buckled and her legs wobbled as if made from rubber.

Jase caught her elbow, supporting her while she struggled to stand upright. "Guess it has been a while since you've ridden."

"Too long," she moaned pitifully.

Chuckling, he took her reins and tethered her horse next to his. "Come on inside. You can stretch out on the couch."

The promise of soft cushions was the inducement she needed to find the strength to follow him inside.

"I'm going to grab a quick shower," he said as he continued on to a bedroom visible through an open door on the opposite side of the large room.

Her gaze already fixed on the overstuffed leather sofa, Mandy fluttered a hand. "I'll be right here," she said, and limped to the sofa. She started to lower herself down, but only made it half-way before the muscles in her legs staged a revolt. Wincing, she braced a hand against the sofa's arm to lever herself back up. "Or maybe I won't," she muttered.

Hoping to work out some of the stiffness, she began to walk around the room. By the third round, the pain had subsided enough for her to become curious of her surroundings. Noticing a group of photographs on the wall, she stopped to study them. Each featured Jase, along with his mom and dad, and created a pictorial history of the Calhoun family. In the first, a young Mrs. Calhoun stood next to her husband, her expression radiant as she cradled an infant Jase in her arms. Jase was probably seven or eight in the second, judging by the missing front teeth his grin revealed. His mother and father stood behind him, and his father had his hands braced on Jase's shoulders, as if to keep his son still.

Amused by Jase's mischievous expression, Mandy shifted her gaze to the third and her heart softened at the sight of Jase's dad. She touched a finger to his face, knowing the picture was taken shortly before his death. He looked so vibrant, so happy posed with his family, it was hard to believe that a freak encounter with an eighteen-wheeler on an icy highway would soon rob him of his life.

Saddened by the memory, she shifted her gaze to include Mrs. Calhoun. They were such a happy couple, she thought, their love and loyalty for each other obvious to even a casual observer. She'd always envied them their relationship and had hoped she'd have a marriage like theirs, one strong enough to last a lifetime.

As it turned out, Mandy's had lasted less than four years.

She heard footsteps and glanced over to find Jase striding toward her, still dressed in the dirty clothes he'd worn all day.

"I thought you were going to take a shower," she said in puzzlement.

"I am," he said, and continued on to the kitchen. "Thought I'd grab a beer while the water's heating up. Want one?"

Shaking her head, she turned her gaze back to the wall of photos. "No, thanks."

He popped the top off the can, tossed it in the waste basket, then moved to stand beside her. "Handsome devil, wasn't I?"

She hid a smile. "To be honest, I hadn't noticed. I was looking at your mom and dad and thinking how happy they look."

He took a sip of his beer and shrugged. "They were happy."

She angled her head to look at him curiously. "You seem to take it for granted. Their happiness, I mean. Not all couples are, you know."

"Believe me, they had their share of spats. But they managed to find a way to work through them."

"I'm surprised you never married."

"Why's that?"

She shrugged. "Because of your parents' example. Men raised in unhappy homes have all kinds of hang-ups about marriage that you wouldn't have. Take Bubba for instance," she said. "He always swore he'd never get married, and I doubt he would've, if Jeannie hadn't gotten pregnant. Not that he doesn't love her," she was quick to add. "Bubba's crazy about Jeanie. But I don't think he would've have taken the plunge as young as he did, if she hadn't gotten pregnant."

"Because of your parents' divorce?"

"Not the divorce precisely. It was the years of fighting that preceded it that turned Bubba off marriage."

"You were raised in the same house he was, yet you married."

"Yeah, but it's different for women."

He slanted her a look. "Is this one of those Venus versus Mars things?"

"No," she said, laughing. "It's just that women are

more emotional than men. And because they are, they're a lot more likely to buy into the idea of happily-ever-after."

"I take it you married for love."

"Yes."

"Do you still love him?"

She shook her head. "No. He destroyed whatever feelings I had for him."

"How?"

"He had an affair. *Multiple* affairs," she clarified, then frowned. "It's true what they say about the wife being the last to know. I wasn't even aware there was anything wrong with our marriage, until I read the letter he left."

"A letter?" He humphed. "Sounds to me like your ex was a coward."

"And a liar and a cheat and a—" Realizing her volume was rising right along with her temper, she stopped to inhale a deep breath, and shook her head. "It doesn't matter. Not any longer."

"Are you sure?" he asked doubtfully. "Just talking about him gets you all stirred up. Passion like that's gotta come from somewhere. If not love, then what?"

She pointed to her hair. "Temper. It goes with being a redhead."

"A trait you share with your brother. Bubba's temper got him into more fights than I care to remember. *And* me, since I always had his back."

She tipped her head to the side and studied Jase thoughtfully.

"What?"

She shook her head. "I was just wondering what traits you and your sister might share?"

"I don't have a sister."

He turned away and she was certain she'd angered him again by mentioning his sister, but after only three steps, he turned around and caught her hand. "Come on," he said, and gave her a tug.

"We're leaving?" she said in confusion, as she hurried to keep up. "I thought you were going to take a shower."

"I am," he replied. "With you."

Five

Jase didn't believe in living life by a set of rules. What few he allowed himself regarded women. He didn't have a problem sleeping with one. Might even stay afterwards to cuddle awhile. But he made damn sure he was gone before morning.

Staying the night with a woman signaled a commitment, intended or not. And Jase wasn't into commitment. No way. He wasn't thirty and single by accident. He never took chances with a woman. He always used protection, even when a woman assured him it wasn't necessary, and he never tangled with one who was looking for anything more than a good time, because that's all he was willing to give in exchange.

He'd broken the overnight rule with Red the night it had rained. But, hell, what fool would go out in a storm like that? He'd come close to breaking it again after showering with her at his cabin. Naked, warm and sated it was awfully tempting to just tuck her into bed beside him and call it a night. Thankfully he'd come to his senses in the nick of time and had escorted her back to his parent's house and left her there to settle in.

But after he returned to his cabin and climbed into his own bed, he couldn't get Red off his mind. He found himself replaying the shower scene over and over in his mind and had gotten hard as a rock. Mad at himself for not being able to control his thoughts, he'd rolled from bed and taken a cold shower. But when he slid beneath the covers again, the image of Red was right there waiting for him, filling his mind—as well as his body—with the kind of needs only a woman could satisfy.

Swearing, he rolled from bed again, jerked on his jeans and T-shirt and grabbed his boots. He hopped across his bedroom on one foot while he tugged on the first, then switched to the other foot in the den and tugged on the second. By the time he reached his truck, he was fully dressed.

He didn't plan to stay that way for long.

Mandy sat up in bed, sure that it was a sound that had awakened her. She strained, listening, and heard footsteps in the hallway. It had to be Jase, she told herself. She distinctly remembered locking all the doors before going to bed.

Or had she?

The bedroom door creaked open.

"Red? You awake?"

Recognizing Jase's voice, she blew out the breath she'd been holding and said dryly, "I am now."

He smiled sheepishly. "Sorry. Couldn't sleep, so I thought I'd check on you. This being your first night alone here, and all…" He lifted a hand, let it drop. "Well, I thought you might be scared."

"I wasn't, but I appreciate the thought."

"You know, it was thoughts of you that were keeping me awake."

Something in his voice made her pulse kick. "What kind of thoughts?" she asked hesitantly.

"Us in the shower. Our bodies slicked with soap." He started across the room. "The steam swirling around us. The heat."

As he stopped beside the bed, she had to tip back her head to keep her gaze on his. "Yeah," she said, and gulped. "It was like a sauna in there."

Hiding a smile, he placed a finger in the hollow of her throat and trailed it down her chest. "The steam wasn't all that was hot. You were, too."

A shiver chased down her spine as his finger settled in the valley between her breasts. "Keep this up, and I will be again."

He lifted a brow. "Promise?"

With his gaze fixed on hers, he peeled his T-shirt over his head and reached for the snap of his jeans.

After that first nocturnal visit, Mandy never had to worry about Jase sneaking into the house in the middle of the night again. Why would she, when he was right there in bed beside her?

While the new sleeping arrangement resolved one worry, it presented her with a new one to puzzle over.

Why was Jase sleeping with her at his parents' house rather than at his own cabin?

The obvious explanation was for the sex, but that didn't make sense. Not totally. There were plenty of nights when they didn't make love and he seemed content to fall asleep with her cuddled in his arms. Was it loneliness that drew him to her bed? she wondered. A need for family? The latter made sense, as Jase had lived and worked alongside his parents all of his adult life. His mother's passing had created a void in his life that Mandy had unwittingly filled—not that Jase and his mother's relationship was sexual. She shuddered at the very thought. But they'd spent a lot of time together, especially after his father's death, sharing meals, talking about business. It was only natural that he would miss the closeness and companionship of family.

Another woman might have been insulted at the idea that Jase was using her as a replacement for family. But not Mandy. She had no preconceived notions or hopes about her relationship with Jase. She might be dangerously close to falling in love with him, if not already there, but she wasn't foolish enough to believe he shared her feelings.

Her mother had referred to him as a womanizer, and Mandy supposed there was probably a bit of truth to her claim. But to Mandy the term held an evil connotation or, at the very least, hinted at a disrespect, and she didn't believe Jase's intentions with any woman, herself included, were anything but innocent. Sexual, yes, but what he offered a woman was an equal exchange of pleasure for pleasure. No promises, no expectations. Just satisfying sex.

And the sex was certainly satisfying, she thought with a shiver. She couldn't argue that, and she doubted Jase would, either. And when it came time for her to leave, she knew he'd just find another woman—or women—to satisfy his sexual needs.

But who would he turn to meet those that only family can provide?

She cut a glance at the adoption file that sat on the corner of her desk, untouched since the day she'd shown it to Jase. He *had* family, she thought stubbornly. It was just a matter of tracking them down.

But how would she ever convince him to search for his family, when he refused to even acknowledge their existence?

Her eyes sharpened. He wouldn't have to search for them, she realized. She would do the searching for him! Finding his birth parents wouldn't be easy. Not when the only information to work with was over thirty years old. She shifted her gaze to the computer on the opposite corner of the desk, knowing the Internet would be the logical place to start her search. Catching her lower lip between her teeth, she glanced around to make sure she was alone, then clicked the link that would take her to Worldwide Web.

While waiting for it to connect, she drew Jase's adoption file in front of her and pulled out the letter from his birth mother. With only a name and state to guide her, she typed in "Barbara Jordan North Carolina" in the search box, and clicked Go. Stunned when her search revealed over a million results, she quickly clicked the link that narrowed it to those listed in the phonebook.

"Nineteen," she murmured, and sank back against her chair, considering the list. There was always the chance that his birth mother had married and would no longer use the name Jordan. Or she might have moved and lived in a totally different state.

Blowing out a breath, she straightened and reached for the mouse again to highlight the list.

"You gotta start somewhere," she muttered and clicked print.

Mandy decided not to tell Jase about her search for his mother. She'd wait until she had located her, then break the news. Calling all the Barbara Jordans on the list was going to take time. To complicate matters, she could only work on her secret project while he was away from the house.

She had just finished one call and was about to make a second when the doorbell rang. Groaning at the interruption, she pushed back from her desk and hurried to the front door.

When she opened it, she blinked in surprise, then screamed, "Bubba!" and flung herself into her brother's arms.

"Dang, Sis," he said, laughing. "If I'd known I'd get this kind of reception, I'd have come sooner."

She held his face between her hands, and simply looked at him, unable to believe he was really there. "What are you doing here? Why didn't you call? Does Jase know you're in town?"

Laughing, he pulled her hands down to hold. "Which question do you want me to answer first?"

"All of them." Almost giddy with excitement, she looped her arm through his and tugged him into the house. "Do you want something to drink? A beer?"

"Beer sounds good." He looked around as he walked with her to the kitchen. "Where's Jase?"

"Out on the ranch somewhere. He should be in soon." She released her hold on him to open the refrigerator. "Where are Jeanie and the kids?"

"Back in Montana. I was in Texas on business, so I thought I'd swing through and see how you and Mother were getting along."

She winced, as she handed him a beer. "I take it you've talked to her."

"As a matter of fact, I have." He took a sip, and studied her. "How long are you two going to carry on this silent war?"

She ducked into the refrigerator for another beer, deciding she was going to need it if they were going to discuss their mother. "Ask her," she grumbled, as she twisted off the cap. "She's the one who started it."

"And it's up to you to end it. She never will."

Knowing what he said was true, she dropped her gaze and dragged a finger along the lip of her bottle. "She doesn't like Jase."

He shrugged. "That's nothing new."

The back door opened and they both turned as Jase stepped inside. He let a whoop when he saw Bubba and started for him, a hand extended in greeting. "Man, it's been a while. Why didn't you let me know you were coming to town? I'd have thrown a party."

"Didn't know I was," Bubba replied. He slanted Mandy a look, then shifted his gaze to Jase again. "Mother called."

Jase's smile faded. "Oh." Before he could say anything more, Bubba reared back and nailed him with a mean right to the jaw.

Caught off guard, Jase stumbled back a step. "Damn, Bubba," he complained, working his jaw to make sure it wasn't broken. "What did you go and do that for?"

Bubba flexed his fingers. "Defending my sister's honor."

Stunned by her brother's actions, Mandy finally found her voice. "My honor doesn't need defending!" she cried.

Bubba took a sip of his beer, then backhanded the moisture from his mouth. "Mother seems to think so."

She dropped her face to her hands with a moan, then snapped her head up to glare at him. "You apologize right now, Bubba Rogers," she said furiously.

"For what?"

"For hitting Jase!"

"He knows it wasn't personal." He glanced at Jase. "Isn't that right, buddy?"

"Depends," Jase replied.

Bubba did a double-take, obviously surprised that Jase hadn't immediately confirmed his statement. "On what?"

"On if you have a problem with Red staying here with me."

Bubba frowned a moment, then glanced at Mandy. "Is he keeping you here against your will?"

She set her jaw. "I'd like to see him try."

Seemingly satisfied with her answer, Bubba turned back to Jase and shrugged. "No problem from this end."

Jase headed for the refrigerator. "I need a beer."

Mandy put a hand out to stop him. "There isn't any. I took the last one."

He changed direction. "Then let's move this party to the cabin. My refrigerator's stocked."

Mandy started to follow, but Bubba stepped in front of her. "Don't you have something to do?"

"Like what?"

"Like paying our mother a visit."

She sagged her shoulders. "Do I have to?" she whined pitifully.

"I suppose you could wait for her to come to you," he said, then shook his head. "Bad idea. She doesn't have a bobsled."

"Bobsled?" Mandy repeated in confusion.

"Yeah. Since hell will have frozen over, she'd never make it here in her car."

Mandy opened the door to her mother's home and called, "Mother? Are you here?"

She heard a pan drop, the scurrying of feet, then her mother appeared in the hallway. One look at Mandy and she pressed a hand to her lips. "Oh, Mandy."

The tears in her mother's voice made Mandy feel as low as a snake for waiting so long to come and see her.

She forced a smile and stepped inside. "I hope I'm not interrupting anything."

Her mother fluttered her hands. "No, no. I was

just straightening up the kitchen. Bubba was here," she explained, then pursed her lips in disapproval. "And you know how your brother is. Never so much as puts a dish in the sink. I'll bet he dirtied five glasses in the short time he was here. Took a shower, too, and left his wet towel in the middle of the floor."

Mandy had heard the same complaints be-fore…and not always about Bubba. Her mother had harangued Mandy's father for similar misdeeds, as well as a laundry list of others, until he'd grown weary of listening to her harping and moved out.

"Come on back to the kitchen," her mother said. "I have a pot of coffee on. I made it for Bubba," she said as she led the way, "but he didn't stay long enough to drink so much as a cup. He was in and out of here so fast my head is still spinning. Although he did find the time to eat half the cake I'd made for the church bazaar," she added sourly.

Mandy turned her eyes upward in a silent prayer of entreaty. If she survived thirty minutes of listen-ing to her mother complain without tearing out her own hair, she'd consider herself lucky.

It was after ten when Mandy returned to the ranch and found both Jase's and Bubba's trucks gone. Assuming they were at Jase's cabin, she considered joining them—for all of about two seconds—then headed for the house and straight for the tub. The evening with her mother had left her emotionally drained and a hot bath held a lot more appeal than listening to Jase and her brother swap lies.

After a thirty minute soak, she crawled between the covers and switched out the bedside lamp, thinking Jase would probably spend the night at the cabin. What with all the flak he'd caught from her mother and brother over her staying at his ranch, she wouldn't blame him if he decided sleeping with her was more trouble than it was worth.

She was in that twilight zone—more asleep than awake—when she felt a warm body snuggle up behind her and the weight of an arm drape her waist. Awake enough to realize Jase had joined her, she laced her fingers through his. "What did you and Bubba do?" she asked sleepily.

He nuzzled his nose at her neck. "Drank a few beers, shot the bull awhile. That's about it. How'd it go with your mother?"

"As good as can be expected, I guess. She made it clear she still doesn't like me staying here."

"Didn't figure she'd change her mind about that."

She rolled to her back to look at him. "I learned something, though."

His smile soft, he brushed her hair back from her face. "And what was that?"

"That I'll never be able to please her. Nobody can. You know how much she adores Bubba, yet she spent a good hour griping about the messes he'd made while he was home today."

"A woman's particular about her house."

"It's more than that," she said, fully awake now. "Mother's a perfectionist. Can't stand for anything to be out of order. Not in her house *or* her life. That's why my dad left. Nothing he did was ever good enough, no matter how hard he tried to please her."

"No offense, but most folks think he was a saint for putting up with her as long as he did."

"I'm beginning to believe that, too, although Mother has always tried to convince Bubba and I otherwise."

"Bubba figured it out. That's why he moved so far away from her."

"And I did just the opposite," she said wryly. "I moved back home."

"Not home exactly," he reminded her.

"No, but within her reach. But it's going to be okay," she said confidently. "Now that I understand I can never please her, I won't spend so much time trying to win her approval, or feel guilty when I don't."

"Sounds like a plan to me."

"It is," she agreed. Snuggling close, she pressed a kiss beneath his chin and closed her eyes. "Good night, Jase."

"'Night, Red."

Mandy hung up the phone and drew a line through the last Barbara Jordan on her list.

"Now what?" she asked herself. The nineteen names on the list hadn't produced a single clue to Jase's birth mother's whereabouts. Every woman she'd spoken with had denied ever knowing a man by the name of Eddie Davis and not a single one of them had ever been a war correspondent in Vietnam.

Not willing to admit defeat, she studied his birth mother's letter, and tried to think how to widen her search. Her efforts to track down his birth mother hadn't turned up any leads at all, not even a relative for her to pursue.

"That's it!" she cried. She had hit a dead end with his birth mother, but she hadn't even attempted to search for his father. That he was deceased didn't matter. Finding a relative of any kind was what important.

Energized by the idea, she turned to the computer and clicked on the link for the Internet, then typed into the search box "Eddie Davis US Army Vietnam Texas 1973." She knew she'd probably overdone it with the parameters, but hoped that adding every bit of information she knew about Jase's birth father from the beginning would narrow the results.

Her eyes widened in surprise when the screen opened to reveal two links. Holding her breath, she clicked the first and waited for the new screen to appear. When it did, she clapped a hand over her heart, as she stared at the thumbnail picture of the young soldier on the screen. She'd found him. Eddie

Davis. Jase's birth father. The hair, the eyes, the high ridge of cheekbone...the likeness was too strong for him to be anyone other than Jase's father.

With her heart pounding in her chest, she tore her gaze from the picture to read the accompanying text.

Assignment: Vietnam June 1971-December 1971
Rank: E-6
Wounded in battle 21 December 1971. Awarded Purple Heart 29 February 1972, in ceremony held at Ft. Hood, Texas.

She stopped reading to frown. Was he wounded in a battle prior to the one where he was killed? If so, why would the army fly him all the way back to Ft. Hood for the ceremony, then fly him back to Vietnam? Why not just give him the medal in Vietnam?

Giving her head a shake, she focused on the text again.

Honorable Discharge, 17 July 1972

"What?" she said in confusion. Wasn't Honorable Discharge a classification given to soldiers who exited the military under normal circumstances, not those who died during service?

Certain she was right about the classification, she looked at the dates more closely and became even more confused. By her calculations, Eddie would have been alive when Jase was born, which made no sense at all. In the letter his birth mother had written to Jase, she'd said she'd attempted to contact Eddie when she'd found out she was pregnant and was told that he had been killed. But how could that have been true, when Jase was born in April of 1972 and Eddie received an Honorable Discharge in July 1972? Even if his mother hadn't carried him full-term, which was likely considering he was twin, Eddie would have been alive when she'd tried to contact him.

Mandy pressed her fingers against her temples, her head aching from trying to make sense of it all. Heaving a weary sigh, she dropped her hands to her lap and focused on the screen again.

"Whoa," she murmured, when she read the last line on the screen.

To view current contact information for this veteran, click here.

Current? She scanned the link again to make sure she'd read what she thought she'd read. Current. It definitely said current. Had she been right? Was Eddie Davis still alive? Her heart was beating so fast, her pulse sounded like thunder in her ears. Drawing in a deep breath, she clicked the link.

Eddie Davis, 2943 Bernhardt Drive, Dallas, Texas, 214-555-6890.

She fell back in her chair and stared. He's alive. Jase's birth father was alive.

It took a moment for her numbed mind to register the magnitude of her discovery. When it did, she leapt from her chair. She had to find Jase. Tell him what she'd found. Tell him his father was alive.

Six

Mandy found Jase in the orchard sawing fallen limbs from the pecan trees into logs. She rocketed from her car and ran toward him, screaming, "Jase! Jase!" at the top of her lungs.

The loud buzz of the chainsaw deafened him to all other sound, and she was less than twenty feet away before he finally heard her and glanced up.

He took one look at her face, dropped the chainsaw and started running. Gripping her arms, he frantically searched her face. "What's wrong? Are you hurt? Did something happen?"

Realizing by his stricken expression that he thought something awful had happened, she shook her head. "No, no. I'm fine." Unable to contain her excitement another second, she threw her arms around him. "Oh, Jase," she cried. "I found your father. I found him!"

He stiffened, then pulled from her embrace and bent to pick up his chainsaw again. "Dad was never lost."

"Not your *adopted* father. Your *birth* father. He wasn't killed in Vietnam. He's alive!" Remembering that Jase hadn't read the letter from his birth mother, as she had, she grabbed his arm, desperate to make him understand. "In the letter your birth mother wrote, she said the man who fathered you was a soldier in Vietnam. When she found out she was pregnant, she tried to contact him and was told he'd been killed. But he wasn't! I found his name listed on a veterans' site on the Internet, with contact information and everything. He lives in Dallas."

He yanked the cord on the chainsaw and the engine roared to life. "My father's buried at Memorial Gardens Cemetery."

Unable to believe he would continue to refuse to acknowledge his birth father, even after learning that he was still living, she hit the kill switch on the machine. "What is wrong with you?" she cried in frustration. "Why do you insist upon acting as if your birth father never existed?"

"Because he didn't," he said flatly.

"But, Jase—"

He threw down the chainsaw and whirled to face her, his face flushed with anger.

"Would you just leave this alone?" he yelled. "As far as I'm concerned, my life began the day Jason and Katie Calhoun brought me to this ranch. *They* are the ones who loved me and raised me. Whoever was involved prior to my adoption doesn't matter. Not to me."

She drew back a step. "I—I'm sorry. I didn't mean to upset you."

He dropped his chin to his chest. "No," he said, shaking his head. "I'm the one who should be apologizing. Not you." He lifted his head and met her gaze again. "It's not you I'm mad at." He caught her hands in his and gave them a pleading squeeze. "Just leave this alone, Red. Okay? I don't want to find those people. They mean nothing to me."

Those people?

If there was a more insensitive way to refer to one's family, Mandy didn't know what it would be.

But Jase had at least acknowledged their existence, she reminded herself as she carried the mail into the house the next day. It was a small victory, but one that brought her a step closer toward her goal of reuniting him with his birth family.

Seating herself behind the desk, she began to go through the day's mail, sorting it into piles, according to its importance. She reached the last envelope and was surprised to find her own name typed across the front. Though she'd filed a change of address with the postmaster shortly after moving to the ranch, this was the first piece of mail she had received there. Curious to know who the letter was from, she glanced at the return address and saw that it was from the office of the Superintendent for the Plano School District.

Realizing it was a response to her application for a teaching position there, she simply stared, unable to bring herself to open it. When she'd agreed to take over Jase's mother's office duties, she'd told him the job was only temporary, as she intended to accept the first teaching position she was offered, even if it required another move. But now faced with the possibility, she wasn't so sure about her decision.

It wasn't that she didn't want to teach. She did. It was the thought of leaving Jase that filled her with dread.

"And aren't you the smug one," she chided herself and ripped open the envelope. "Assuming it's an offer, when it could as easily be a rejection."

But when she unfolded the letter and read the first paragraph, she discovered she was wrong on both counts, as it was neither an offer or a rejection. It was a request for an interview.

Which was almost as bad as receiving an offer, she thought miserably. If she put off responding to the request, she was taking a chance on someone else getting the job. Turnover for business teachers was low, and when an opening came up, it was generally snapped up within days of being announced. If there was even the slightest chance she would receive an offer to teach in San Saba, she'd wouldn't bother with interviewing for the position in Plano. But if there wasn't...

Catching her lower lip between her teeth, she slid a glance at the phone. She supposed she could call San Saba's superintendent and ask him if he thought he'd have a position available in the fall. But would that appear too pushy? she wondered. Too desperate?

"So what if it does," she muttered and reached for the phone. "The worst he can do is say no."

Where I land depends on who offers me a position first.

She slowly lowered the phone back to the cradle, remembering her flippant response to Jase's query about her staying in San Saba to teach. At the time, she really hadn't cared where she taught school, as long as it wasn't in Corpus Christi, where her ex still lived. But now the thought of leaving San Saba—or more importantly, Jase—made her feel physically ill.

"Hey, Red. Is that today's mail?"

She glanced up to find Jase strolling into the office and forced a smile. "Sure is. Were you expecting something?"

"Yeah. I talked to one of my pecan buyers this

morning and he said he sent me the name of another guy who's interested in buying some of my fall crop."

"Calhoun Pecan Orchard's mail is there in the middle," she said, gesturing to the pile.

He scooped it up and thumbed through it as he rounded the desk.

When he reached her side, he nudged her leg with his knee.

She looked up at him in confusion. "What?"

"Get up."

She frowned at him as she rose. "If you wanted to sit down to read your mail, you could have used the couch. I do have work, you know."

He slid onto the chair she'd vacated, then hooked an arm around her waist and pulled her down to his lap. "Yeah, but then you would've had to walk all the way over there to sit on my lap. I was just saving you some steps."

"Well, aren't you the thoughtful one," she said dryly.

He nuzzled her cheek with his. "I like to think so." He tipped his head at the letter on her desk. "What's that?"

She splayed a hand across the page to prevent him from reading it. "Nothing. Just some mail I received today."

He goosed her in the ribs. "What is it? A letter from your boyfriend?"

"Not even close."

"Let me see it." Before she could stop him, he snatched the letter from beneath her hand.

"Jase!" she cried, and tried to grab it back.

Holding it out of her reach, he read aloud:

Dear Ms. Rogers,

I've reviewed your application for a teaching position in the Plano school district, and was very impressed with your level of experience, as well as the references you provided. The next step in the hiring process is an interview. Unfortunately, the telephone number you listed on your application is no longer a working number. Please call me at your earliest convenience so that we can schedule a time for us to meet.

He glanced her way. "Does this mean you got the job?"

She took the letter from him and carefully refolded it, avoiding his gaze. "No. I have to pass the interview first."

"Is there a chance you wouldn't?"

She lifted a shoulder. "I suppose."

"In other words, the job is yours once the interview is over."

"Not necessarily," she said, though she knew, with her credentials, she'd have to really bomb on the interview for the superintendent not to offer her the position.

"Is this what you want? The job in Plano, I mean."

Unsure how much of her feelings to reveal to him, she shook her head. "I don't know. I want to teach. There's no question about that. But I've enjoyed living in San Saba again, and I'm not sure I want to move to another town."

"Then don't," he stated emphatically. "Teach here."

"They haven't offered me a job."

"Oh."

"Yeah. Oh."

He frowned thoughtfully for a moment, then lifted her from his lap and stood. "Well, don't start packing yet. Who knows? San Saba may come through with an offer yet."

Mandy didn't start packing, but she did call the superintendent's office in Plano and scheduled an appointment for her interview. Due to the length of time it had taken the superintendent to get I touch with her, he requested they meet as soon as possible. Though she would've preferred to put off the interview as long as possible, in hopes she'd receive another offer closer to San Saba, she had a little choice but agree to meet with him the next day.

She rose early on the day of the appointment and went to her office, needing to prepare the payroll checks before she left for Dallas.

She'd just shutdown the computer when Jase strode in.

"Perfect timing," she said and handed him the envelopes containing the checks. "I just finished making payroll."

"Thanks," he said as he slid the envelopes into his back pocket. "About ready to go?"

She forced a smile. "Ready as I'll ever be."

"Nervous?"

"A little," she admitted.

He slipped his arms around her waist. "If you don't want to go, then don't."

Finding it much too tempting to sink into his embrace and forget about her appointment in Dallas, she shifted away. "I have to. I'd be a fool to let this opportunity pass."

"Yeah, I suppose you're right," he agreed reluctantly.

She picked up her purse. "I might not get back until late. There's a casserole in the refrigerator for your dinner."

"Thanks." He bussed her a quick kiss, then started out, but stopped in the doorway and glanced back. "I'd wish you luck, but that'd be the same as wishing bad luck on myself."

"How's that?"

"If you pass the interview—" he gave the computer a pointed glance "—that means I'll be butting heads with that damn machine again."

"Well, thanks a lot," she said, feigning indignation.

Grinning, he shot her a wink, then was gone.

She heard the front door close behind him, and sighed, knowing she'd put off leaving as long as she could. She glanced around the office one last time and her eyes settled on the adoption folder lying on the corner of her desk. She hesitated a moment, then scooped it up and headed out.

"Hey, Henry," Jase said, and extended his hand in greeting.

Henry pumped his hand enthusiastically. "Good to see you, Jase. It's been a while." He gave Jase a hopeful look. "Does this mean you've reconsidered my suggestion that you run for the School Board?"

Chuckling, Jase shook his head. "No, sir. Board and bored have too much in common for me to even consider tossing my hat into the ring. I'll leave that spot open for someone better suited for the job."

The superintendent gestured for Jase to take a seat, then settled behind his desk again. "A shame, if you ask me. No one cares more about the welfare of the citizens of San Saba than you."

"I appreciate that, Henry, but my answer's still no."

Henry shrugged. "Well, if I can't convince you to run for the School Board, what can I do for you today?"

Jase settled his hat on his thigh. "To be honest, I'm here to ask for a favor."

The superintendent opened his hands. "Name it and I'll do what I can."

Jase shifted uneasily in his chair. "Well, it's like this. I have a friend who's looking for a teaching job."

Henry reached down to open a drawer. "I've got an application right here. Just have your friend—"

Jase held up a hand. "She's already got an application on file."

Henry drew his hand back to rest on the desk. "And what is this friend's name?"

"Mandy Rogers."

"Yes, indeed," Henry said, smiling. "One of our own. And quite an impressive young lady, I might add. San Saba would be lucky to have a teacher like her in our schools."

"So you're going to offer her a job?" Jase asked hopefully.

Henry shook his head with regret. "Wish I could. But we don't have any positions open at the moment."

"She mentioned the slow turnover for business teachers, but surely you could find a spot for her until one opens up. She's sharp as a tack. I bet she could teach just about any subject and do a damn fine job of it."

"I'm sure she could," Henry agreed. He swiveled his chair around, lifted a tall stack of papers from the credenza, then turned and dropped them on the center of his desk. "These are the applications currently on file. I place them in the order I receive them, with the oldest on the top and the most recent going to the bottom. Even if I was willing to move Ms. Rogers application to the top, which I would as a favor to you, I don't have an opening for her. I filled all the teaching positions before school ended in May."

Heaving a sigh, Jase stood and extended his hand. "I appreciate your time, Henry."

"I'm keeping her application active," Henry assured him. "If anything comes up…"

Jase nodded and turned for the door, knowing how slim that possibility was. "Thanks, Henry."

Mandy searched each street sign she passed, wishing she'd taken the time to print a map from the Internet before leaving the house that morning. With nothing more to guide her than the scribbled notes she'd taken when she'd stopped at a service station to ask for directions, she feared she'd never find Eddie Davis's house.

She'd been driving since she'd finished her interview an hour earlier and she wasn't any closer to locating his home than she was when she'd started out. But she wasn't giving up, she promised herself. Jase wouldn't appreciate what she was about to do, but that was just too bad. Eddie Davis had a right to know he'd fathered a son.

Even if that son wanted nothing to do with his father.

Eddie might not be happy with her, either, she thought with a niggle of apprehension. She'd thought about calling him first, but had decided that, considering what she wanted to share with him, a face-to-face meeting was necessary. She had no idea how he would take the news and was afraid, not knowing anything about his health, that a shock like this could bring on a heart attack or stroke, which could be fatal, if he received the news over the phone and lived alone.

She slowed, her heart kicking into a faster beat, as she spotted the sign for Bernhardt Drive. No turning back now, she told herself nervously, and turned right onto the street, searching the numbers painted on the curb for 2943.

Finding the address, she parked in front and leaned across the seat to peer up at the house. Probably built in the eighties, the one-story brick blended nicely with the other homes in the neighborhood, yet it lacked something she couldn't quite put her finger on.

She blew out a breath, grabbed the file folder and climbed from her car. With each step that drew her closer to the front door, her breath grew shorter and shorter, her hands damp with perspiration. Gathering her courage, she punched the bell, then stepped back to wait.

She was about to punch it a second time, when the

door swung open and a man stepped into the opening. Rendered speechless by his likeness to Jase, she could only stare.

His mouth dipped into a frown. "If you're selling something, we have a 'No Solicitation' policy in this neighborhood."

She gave herself a shake. "No, no," she hurried to assure him. "I'm not selling anything. This is strictly a social visit."

His frown deepened and he tipped his head to look at her more closely. "Am I supposed to know you?"

Laughing softly, she shook her head. "No, but I know you Mr. Davis. Or rather, of you," she clarified, and extended her hand. "I'm Mandy Rogers."

He studied her as they shook, then opened the door wider, obviously deciding she didn't appear to pose a threat. "Come on in," he said and led the way back to what she assumed was his den.

She noticed that he walked with a slight limp, which she hoped wasn't an indication that he did have a health problem, as she'd feared. Although that's what had made her decide to break the news to him in person, rather than over the phone, she wasn't at all sure she'd know how to handle a medical emergency, should one present itself.

"Excuse the mess," he said, as he dropped down onto a recliner. "This is the maid's day off."

She glanced around, noting the foot-high stack of

newspapers piled beside his chair and the gray film of dust that lay on top of the television opposite it and bit back a smile, relieved to discover that he had a sense of humor. "Your home looks...comfortable."

"And you don't," he replied, and waved a hand. "Sit, sit. I hate looking up at a person when they're talking."

Charmed by his gruff personality, she seated herself on the sofa near his chair.

He narrowed an eye at her. "You said you know of me. Mind explaining how?"

Her nerves returned, a trembling reminder of the purpose of her visit. Drawing in a steadying breath, she settled the file on her lap. "I found you on the Internet."

"Had to be looking. It's not like I advertise myself there."

"Oh, I was definitely looking for you."

"Why?"

"It's a long and complicated story."

He opened a hand. "Time's all I have, since I retired, so let's hear it."

"You served in Vietnam."

"Me and about a million other soldiers." He expression turned suspicious. "Is that what this is about? Are you a reporter or something, looking for a new angle to report on this war in Iraq?"

"Oh, no, sir," she assured him. "I'm a school teacher, not a reporter."

"I'm not interested in sharing my experiences in Vietnam with a classroom of kids."

"That's not why I'm here."

"Then why *are* you here?" he demanded to know.

"If you'll give me a minute, I can explain." She drew in another breath, trying to think how to tell him all she'd discovered about his past, things he didn't even know himself.

"If my information is correct," she said, "you spent one of your leaves in Saigon."

His face turned to stone, much like Jase's did when he didn't want to talk about a particular subject.

"How do you know that?"

"I…I read it in a letter." Realizing there was no easy way to break the news to him, she opened the file and pulled out the letter Jase's birth mother had written. She stretched out a hand, offering it to Eddie.

He eyed it suspiciously, but made no move to take it.

"I believe you know the lady who wrote it," she said quietly. "Barbara Jordan."

His entire body jerked as if he'd received an electrical shock. "Barbara?" he repeated in a choked voice.

She gulped, nodded. "She wrote the letter to her son."

He gripped his hands over the recliners' arms and pushed himself back deeper into the cushion, as if to distance himself from the letter. "Whatever she had to say to her son is no business of mine."

"Yes, it is," she insisted and pushed the letter at him again. "In fact the majority of the letter is about you."

He continued to eye the letter as if it was a snake that was about to bite him.

"Would you rather I read it to you?" she offered softly.

He jerked his gaze to hers at her offer and she saw the dread in his eyes, the pain. She thought for a moment he was going to refuse, possibly even demand that she leave, but after a long moment, he bobbed his chin once, granting her permission.

Her hands trembled as she drew the letter before her and began to read:

To my son,

I'm a writer by trade, yet I can't seem to find the words to express what's in my heart, to share with you the things I want you to know.

Above all else, please know that giving you up is the hardest thing I've ever done in my life.

"Hold on a minute."

She glanced up at Eddie.

"Barbara didn't keep her son?"

"No, she gave him up for adoption."

He shook his head. "Then, you've got the wrong person. The Barbara I knew would never do that. If she had a child, she'd keep it. She'd never give it away to a stranger."

She moved to kneel at his feet and placed a hand on his knee. "No. I have the right person. If you'll let me continue, I think you'll understand."

When he offered no further argument, she began to read again.

From the moment I felt the first butterfly wings of movement in my womb, I loved you with all my heart.

I'm an unwed mother, but please don't think badly of me or your father. Ours was not a sordid affair. I met your father in Vietnam. He was an American soldier on a three-day leave of duty—

"No. Oh, God no."

Mandy looked up to find Eddie had dropped his face to his hands. Knowing by his reaction that he realized now that he was the father of Barbara's child, she rubbed a soothing hand over his knee.

"I know this must come as a shock," she said softly.

He dropped his hands to look at her in disbelief. "A shock? I fathered a child, for God's sake. A son!" He pushed from the chair to glare down at her. "I'm not shocked, dammit. I'm mad! She had no right to keep this from me."

She rose and laid a calming hand on his arm. "You need to hear the rest. Once you do, you'll understand why she did what she did."

He jerked his arm away. "No I won't. There's no excuse for what she did. I have a son, dammit! A son. And she kept him from me."

"I know, I know," she soothed, then refolded the letter, giving up on being able to read it to him. It was better to just blurt it out and get it over with.

"She thought you were dead," she said.

Having paced away, he whipped his head around to look at her. "Dead?" he repeated, then turned, flinging his arms out wide. "Do I look dead to you?"

Hiding a smile, she shook her head. "No, sir, Mr. Davis. You look very much alive to me."

He dropped his arms to scowl. "Eddie. Call me, Eddie." He flipped a hand, indicating the letter. "Since you know more about me than I know about myself, seems we ought to be on a first name basis."

"Okay…Eddie."

"So what in the hell gave her the idea I was dead?" he asked, his anger returning.

"When she found out she was pregnant, she tried to contact you and was told by the military that you were killed in battle."

Swearing, he whirled to pace again. "Damn war," he muttered. "I was *wounded* in battle, not killed."

"I wondered about that," she said. "After I discovered that you were alive, I mean. I didn't understand why she was told you were killed."

He dragged a hand over his hair, then dropped it with a weary sigh. "You would if you'd been there.

Things were crazy over there. By that time, some of our troops were being pulled out and shipped back home, yet the fighting was still going on. Those responsible for reporting casualties didn't always get the information right. Took weeks, sometimes months to get them corrected." He sank down onto the recliner, his mind taking him back.

"We were out in the field," he said. "Ran into a band of Vietcong. We were outnumbered, but not by much. They had a lot of fire power, but nothing we couldn't handle. Figured we'd kick some butt and head back to camp. Already had them on the run." He glanced up at her and grimaced. "Then we discovered the retreat was a trick. They'd drawn us into a mine field. Toe-poppers we called them," he said, then reached down to hike up the leg of his pants. "Blew my foot clean off."

Mandy stared, the cause for the limp she'd noticed earlier now obvious.

His scowl deepening, he dropped the leg of his pants to hide the prosthesis. "As soon as the first mine exploded, those Cong turned back on us, then it was the Americans running." He shook his head sadly. "I didn't blame the guys for leaving me behind. They thought I was dead." He snorted a breath. "Hell, *I* thought I was dead."

"So that's why Barbara was told you were killed?" she asked.

"Probably. I was reported as killed in action, but that was changed after they found me. If it was during that time in between when she tried to contact me, they would've told her I was dead."

She looked at him curiously. "How did you manage to survive, if you were left behind?"

"My team came back for me. I knew they would eventually. We always collected the bodies, if at all possible. Once I knew the enemy was far enough away that they wouldn't see me, I dragged myself into the jungle and hid."

Fascinated by his story, she asked, "How long did you have to wait?"

"Two days." He looked down his nose at her. "Longest two days of my life, I can tell you that. Felt more like an eternity."

She blew out a breath, easily able to imagine how frightened he must have been. "I'm sure it did."

"Here," he said, and held out his hand. "Let me see the letter."

Mandy gave it to him, then sank down at his feet again while he read it.

By the time he reached the last line, tears were running down his face.

Her heart breaking for him, she laid a comforting hand on his knee. "I'm so sorry, Eddie."

He dragged the back of his hand across his eyes and sniffed. "Yeah. Me, too." He dropped the letter to his lap. "She said there were twins. A girl and a boy. But the letter's written to only the boy. What happened to the other baby?"

"I don't know. Evidently they were adopted into different homes. I only know Jase, your son."

"My son," he said, then dragged a hand down his face, as if still having a hard time adjusting to the fact that he'd fathered one child, much less two. "What's he like?"

She smiled softly. "A lot like you. You have the same hair color. Similar build."

"Where does he live?"

"San Saba."

His eyes shot wide. "San Saba! As in San Saba, Texas?"

She nodded.

"Damn," he murmured. "To think I've lived alone all these years and had a son living a couple of hours away."

"More like three hours," she corrected, then glanced at her watch and rose. "And I better get going or it'll be midnight before I get home."

"You live in San Saba, too?"

"Yes." She hesitated a moment, unsure how to explain her relationship with Jase, but realized it was impossible to explain something she didn't understand herself, and said instead, "I'm currently living in the house your son grew up in."

His gaze on hers, he braced his hands against the chair's arms and stood. "Can I see him?"

She was slow to answer, feeling Eddie had suffered enough disappointments in one day. "I don't know," she said hesitantly and moved to pick up the folder containing Jase's adoption papers. "Jase has always known he was adopted, but he only recently learned the circumstances of his birth. He really hasn't had a chance to—"

He held up a hand. "You don't need to explain. Obviously he wants nothing to do with me. If he did, he'd be here, instead of you."

She ducked her head, unable to bear the sadness in his eyes. "Maybe in time," she began.

He laid a hand on her shoulder. "I don't blame him for the way he feels and I don't want you to blame him, either. If I were him, I'd probably hate me, too."

She snapped up her head. "Oh, he doesn't hate you."

Smiling, he draped his arm along her shoulder and walked with her to the door. "Hate's an awfully strong word, but I'll bet it comes mighty close to describing how he feels about me."

Mandy stopped to face him. "I know this is asking a lot, since you don't know me or anything, but would you mind if I stayed in contact with you?"

His smile warmed. "I don't mind at all. In fact, I hope you will."

She breathed a sigh of relief. "Thanks. I may be moving here soon, and it would be nice to know I have a friend in the area."

He dropped his chin, nodding, then looked up at her from beneath his brow. "Would it be okay if I hugged you?"

Tears rushed to her eyes and she nodded.

He wrapped his arms around her and hugged her tight. As he held her she sensed the loneliness in him, the regret.

When he withdrew, he dragged a hand beneath his nose. "I appreciate you coming here. It took a lot of courage to tell me the things you did."

Choked by emotion, she could only nod. "I'd better go."

She'd reached the edge of the porch, when he called out to stop her.

"Mandy?"

She turned. "Yes?"

"You didn't say anything about contacting Barbara. Do you know where she is? What she's doing?"

She shook her head. "No, I'm sorry, I don't. I searched for her on the Internet, too, and called every Barbara Jordan in North Carolina, but none of them were her."

He nodded gravely, then lifted a hand in farewell. "Be careful driving home."

Seven

It was well after midnight by the time Mandy made it back to the ranch. Throughout the drive from Dallas, she'd debated whether or not she should tell Jase about going to see Eddie. He'd be furious with her. She knew that. But she sincerely believed the two men needed each other. If Jase would only give Eddie a chance, she was sure he would like him. How could he not, when the two were so much alike?

But how would she ever be able to persuade Jase to give Eddie that chance, when he refused to allow her to so much as mention his birth father?

She didn't have an answer to the problem she

faced, but she wasn't giving up. She had to get the two together. For Eddie's sake, as much as Jase's.

Though it was late when she entered the house, a few lights were still on. Unsure if Jase was still up or if he'd left the lights on as a courtesy for her, she called softly, "Jase?" as she tiptoed down the hall. Hearing the television, she followed the sound to the den, where she found Jase asleep on the sofa. She switched off the set, then crossed to the sofa, intending to wake him.

Instead she simply looked down at him, her heart swelling until she was sure it would burst. When had she fallen in love with him? she wondered. She had worshiped the very ground he walked on for as long as she could remember, but the feelings she had for him now were different, stronger, and the thought of leaving him was almost more than she could bear.

She wasn't going to tell him about Eddie tonight, she told herself. Maybe not even tomorrow. As selfish as it might seem, she wanted her last few days with him to be happy ones and without the tension that discussions of his birth parents always drew.

Swallowing back the emotion that filled her throat, she leaned to press a kiss against his forehead.

His eyelids fluttered up and a sleepy smile spread across his lips as he focused on her. "You're home."

The emotion she'd swallowed only moments ago rose again to choke her at the word "home." "Yeah," she managed to say. "Sorry I'm so late."

He hooked an arm around her waist and pulled her down to lie with him. "I was worried."

The absurdity of his claim drew a smile. "I can see that you were," she said dryly.

He lifted his head to look at her. "I was," he insisted. "Wore the soles clean off my boots walking the floor."

"Um-hmm," she hummed doubtfully.

He dropped his head back against the cushion. "Okay," he admitted grudgingly. "So maybe I didn't wear the soles off my boots, but I did worry."

She gave his chest a reassuring pat. "It's the thought that counts."

Smiling, he stroked a hand over her hair. "So how'd the interview go?"

"Okay, I guess."

"Did you get the job?"

Avoiding his gaze, she plucked at a button on his shirt. "I won't know until Friday." She drew in a shuddery breath, deciding she might as well prepare him. "If I do get offered the job, I'll have to move next week."

His hand stilled on her hair. "Next week? That's kinda fast, isn't it?"

She shook her head, but couldn't bring herself to look at him. "Not really. School starts in a couple of weeks. I'll need to get my classroom ready and my lesson plans made."

He remained silent for a long moment, then rolled

from beneath her and scooped her up into his arms. "I don't know about you," he said, as he started for the bedroom. "But I'm exhausted."

That he didn't want to talk about her leaving was obvious. But his claim of exhaustion as his reason for wanting to go to bed was an out-and-out lie. Once there, he didn't even pretend sleep. Instead he made love with Mandy for hours with a tenderness that brought tears to her eyes.

Mandy knew the only way she could get through the next few days was to stay busy. If she did get the teaching position, she wanted to leave Jase's business affairs in order, and that gave her plenty to do. She spent hours creating manuals for each of his businesses, including account information and details of the duties required for her replacement to manage each. She even created a more efficient system for keeping track of the reservations made for the hunting cabins and developed a spreadsheet to monitor income and expenses. The work was tedious, but welcome, as it kept her mind off the phone call she both awaited and dreaded.

When she felt the office was in shape, she started on the house, giving it a good cleaning from top to bottom. As she worked her way from room to room, she tried not to think about the house standing empty, if she should leave. She knew Jase wouldn't stay in his parents' home without her there with him. He'd return to his cabin and the house's beauty would fade over time due to neglect.

She was in the kitchen preparing meals to freeze for Jase, when the telephone rang. She whirled at the sound and stared at the phone. It rang a second time, and she plucked the receiver from its base on the wall.

"Calhoun residence," she said, trying to keep the dread from her voice.

"Mandy Rogers, please."

"This is she."

"Dr. Garrison with the Plano School District. I have good news for you, Ms. Rogers. The Board voted unanimously to accept your application."

She pressed her lips together, to hold back the sob that threatened. "Thank you, Dr. Garrison. And please share my thanks with the Board."

"You have the packet I gave you pertaining to the school you've been assigned?"

She nodded numbly. "Yes. Yes, I have it."

"Good. Well, congratulations. And if you have any questions, give me a call."

"Thank you, Dr. Garrison. I will."

She hung up the phone, then dropped her forehead against the wall and let the tears fall.

Jase stepped into the kitchen and lifted a brow, as his gaze settled on the ornately set table. "What's the occasion?"

Avoiding his gaze, Mandy struck a match and touched the flame to one of the tapers she'd set in the center of the table. "Dr. Garrison called."

"About the teaching job?"

She shifted slightly to light the second candle, praying he wouldn't notice the tremble in her fingers. "Yes. The board accepted my application." She blew out the match, then forced a smile before turning to face him. "Just think. In less than a week, I'll be out of your hair."

Grimacing, he tossed his hat onto the counter and crossed to the table. "You haven't been in my hair."

"That's nice of you to say, but I'm sure it'll be a relief to get back to your own routine."

"Routine? Me?" He snorted a wry laugh. "That'll be the day."

Dropping his gaze, he picked up a fork and dragged the tines along the cloth. "I went to see Henry a couple of days ago."

Hope surged in her chest. "You did?"

"Yeah. Tried to pull a few strings so you could stay in San Saba."

"And…" she prodded.

He dropped the fork and shook his head. "No dice. All the positions were filled before school let out in May."

Which meant her last remaining chance of staying in San Saba was gone.

She wanted to touch him, cling to him, thank him

for trying to help her get a teaching job in San Saba. But more than anything she wanted him to beg her to stay. Knowing that would never happen, she turned away. "You're going to love what we're having for dinner," she said with forced gaiety. "I made all your favorite things."

"Red?"

She paused with her hand on the oven door, and glanced back at him.

He opened his arms. "Come here."

She wanted to believe the gesture was a prelude to him asking her to stay. But she knew Jase better than that. If anything, it was an apology because he couldn't...or wouldn't. Even knowing that, she stepped willingly into his arms. She squeezed her eyes shut tight as he wrapped his arms around her, promising herself she wouldn't cry.

Turning her lips to his cheek, she whispered, "I'm going to miss you."

His arms tightened around her. "I'm going to miss you, too, Red."

Mandy made the decision to leave during the night, knowing that staying any longer was only prolonging the inevitable, as well as the pain. She didn't tell Jase what she planned to do, wanting to save them both an awkward and potentially emotional farewell.

Packing wasn't a problem. She'd lost most of her possessions when the storm destroyed her apartment.

What little was left would fit in her car. The one obstacle she faced was where she would stay once she arrived in Dallas.

Falling back on the only friend she had in the area, she picked up the phone and dialed Eddie's number.

"Eddie, it's Mandy."

"Well, hi," he said, sounding surprised to hear from her so soon. "I wondered if you'd made it home safe."

She gulped back tears at his reference to "home." "Y-yes, I made the drive without any problems." She curled her hand into a fist, knowing she was asking a lot of someone who barely knew her. "Listen, Eddie. I need a favor."

"Whatever it is, it's yours for the asking."

That he would make such an open-ended offer didn't surprise her. Though she'd met him only once, she'd suspected his gruffness hid a warm and generous heart.

"You may regret saying that," she warned.

"Not a chance."

"Well," she began uneasily. "As it turns out, it looks as if I'm going to be moving to Dallas sooner than I expected, and I need a place to stay. Only for a couple of days," she was quick to assure him, so he wouldn't think she was asking to move in permanently. "Just until I have a chance to find a place of my own."

"No problem. I've got two extra bedrooms. One of them is yours for as long as you want."

She released the breath she'd been holding. "Thanks, Eddie."

"So when are you coming?"

She winced, realizing it was short notice. "Today, if that's all right with you."

"Fine with me. I'll roll out the red carpet."

"Thanks, Eddie. I really appreciate this."

After telling him what time to expect her, Mandy hung up the phone and set to work. Jase had left after breakfast for Austin and wasn't due back until later that afternoon, which gave her plenty of time to clear out before he returned.

Packing up her things and loading her car hardly took any time at all and by noon, she was ready to go. She made one last sweep through the house, to make sure she hadn't left anything behind, then went to the office and laid the letter she'd written Jase on top of the desk for him to find.

When she turned for the door again, she pressed a hand against her heart, feeling as if she was leaving half, if not all of it, behind.

"Hey, Red!" Jase called, as he stepped through the backdoor.

Not hearing a response, he tucked the bouquet of roses he bought her to celebrate her new job behind his back and headed for the office, figuring she was still working. But when he entered the room, the lights were off, indicating she'd already quit for the day.

"Where are you, Red?" he shouted and retraced his steps, heading for the bedroom wing of the house. He stuck his head inside the room he'd shared with her and looked around. The bed was made and nothing seemed out of order, yet a shiver of foreboding chased down his spine.

"Red?" he said hesitantly and crossed to peer into the adjoining bath. He found nothing out of place there, either, and that alone was enough to raise an alarm. The bottles and jars of toiletries usually lined up on the counter were gone, as was the toothbrush she kept in a glass to the right of the sink.

Spinning around, he raced back to the office and flipped on the overhead light. He spotted the envelope on the desk and crossed to snatch it up. Written across the front in Red's handwriting was "Jase."

Fearing he knew what was inside, he tossed the bouquet of roses on the desk, ripped open the envelope and pulled out the single sheet of paper inside.

Jase,

I apologize for leaving without at least telling you goodbye, but I probably would've cried if I had, which would have just embarrassed us both.

Thanks so much for all you've done for me—giving me a job I didn't want, a place to stay after the storm flattened my apartment, helping me dig through all the mud and crud for my stuff. But most of all, thanks for being my friend.

I have a confession to make. When I went to Dallas for my interview, I went to see Eddie Davis, your birth father. My purpose in going wasn't to attempt to open a line of communication between the two of you. Although, I think you'd really like him if you ever met him. I know I do. I went to see him, because I felt he had a right to know he had fathered a son.

I wasn't sure what to expect when I saw him, and I was surprised to discover he's a lot like you. Same color hair and eyes, similar build. He even talks with a slow Texas drawl just like yours.

I promised I wouldn't mention your birth parents any more, and I won't after this. If you should ever decide you want to meet them, Eddie's contact information is in the adoption file in the first drawer of the credenza. I wasn't able to find any information on your birth mother, so you're on your own locating her. Now. That's the last time. I promise.

Please don't think I've left you in a bind. All the bills are paid, the filing done. I also made the payroll for this week. You'll find the checks in the safe. And you don't need to worry about training my replacement. I left three manuals of instructions on my desk, one for each of your companies.

The house is clean—for the moment. What

messes you make in the kitchen, you'll have to clean up. There's a week or two of meals in the freezer. After that, you might consider rehiring the housekeeper you thought you no longer needed.

I think that about covers everything.

Thanks again, Jase. You'll never know how much I enjoyed spending part of my summer with you.

Love,

Mandy

P.S. Just so you'll know, I don't kiss my friends the way I kissed you. Not even the male kind.

He read the postscript again, and gave his head a rueful shake. Leave it to Red to figure out a way to get in the last word.

Heaving a sigh, he lowered the letter to stare at the window. He wanted to be mad at her for leaving the way she had, but how could he, when he was to blame for her leaving at all? He would've had to be blind not to see that she didn't want to move to Dallas, to realize that she was in love with him.

And he loved her, too.

But enough to give her what she wanted, what she deserved? Enough to marry her?

Shaking his head, he tossed the letter on the desk beside the bouquet of roses and turned away.

Jase Calhoun simply wasn't the marrying kind.

* * *

As Mandy started up the walk, the door swung wide and Eddie stepped out onto his porch, wearing a welcoming smile.

One look at him and she burst into tears.

He froze, his smile melting, then he was rushing to her side. "Are you all right?" he asked, as he slipped her overnight bag from her shoulder.

She nodded, then shook her head, unable to stop crying.

He grabbed her arm and ushered her toward the house. "Let's get you inside and you can tell me what happened."

"I—it's nothing," she said, trying her best to stem the tears.

"Yeah," he quipped wryly, as he guided her down to the sofa, "and I've got two good feet."

He eased back to sit on the edge his recliner, watching her uneasily. "Want me to go and kick his butt?"

Her eyes shot wide. "What?"

"I would, you know," he said. "Even if he is my son."

That he knew she was crying over Jase was shocking enough to stop her tears. "How did you know?"

He snorted. "I may be an old bachelor, but I've been around enough women to recognize when one's heart is hurting."

"But how did you know it was because of Jase?"

"Caller ID. When you called this morning, the

Calhoun name came up on the screen. Put two and two together…." He shrugged. "Wasn't too hard to figure out the rest."

Fresh tears rose to fill her eyes. "I left without even saying goodbye."

"You don't seem the type who'd do something like that without good reason."

She dropped her chin and dragged a hand beneath her nose. "I had no choice."

He shot to his feet. "He kicked you out? Why, I have a good mind to—"

She patted the air between them. "No, no. It wasn't like that. Leaving was my choice, not his. If I'd stayed, it would've only made it that much harder when it came time for me to leave."

He sank slowly down to his recliner again. "You're in love with him?"

She pressed a hand to her lips and nodded.

"Holy Mother of God," he murmured.

"I know," she said tearfully. "It was a stupid thing to do. I've had a crush on him since I was a little girl, and when I moved back home after my divorce and saw him again…" She opened her hands. "I couldn't help myself. I fell in love with him."

"And he doesn't feel the same for you?"

"Oh, he likes me well enough. Probably loves me in his own way." She shook her head, unable to explain. "You'd have to know Jase to understand."

"I'm not sure I'd want to know a man who'd hurt a girl as sweet as you."

Her tears welled higher that he would think that of her. "That's really nice of you to say, but please don't think badly of Jase. He really is a great guy. I knew all along that I cared more than he did. It's just that I…" She lifted a shoulder. "I guess I let my heart overrule my head."

"Sometimes a person's heart is smarter than his head."

She looked at him curiously, and he flapped a hand. "Hell. Don't listen to me. I'm just an old bachelor. What do I know about love?"

Jase trudged toward the office of the newspaper, sure that he looked like a drunk after pulling a week-long bender. And no wonder. He hadn't a slept a wink since Red left. With her gone, he'd seen no reason to remain at his parents' home, so he'd moved back to his cabin. He blamed the first night's insomnia on him having grown accustomed to the bed in the guestroom of his parents' house. Desperate for sleep, the second night he'd returned to his parents' house and crawled into the guestroom bed. But sleep had still evaded him.

Images of Red hadn't.

Heaving a sigh, he pushed open the door to the newspaper office and approached the cubicle marked "Classifieds." "Excuse me," he said to the clerk busily clicking away at a keyboard. "I need to place an ad."

The woman looked up from her computer screen and dragged off a set of headphones, a smile blooming on her face. "Well, if it isn't Jase Calhoun in the flesh."

He frowned a moment, trying to place the woman.

"Suzy Hopper," she said helpfully. "We dated for a while a couple years back."

He dragged a hand over his hair, embarrassed that he hadn't recognized her. "Sorry. Seems my brain hasn't kicked in yet this morning."

She hid a smile. "You do look a little worse for wear. Must have been one heck of a party."

"Don't I wish," he said miserably. Anxious to get his business over with before he stuck his foot in his mouth again, he pulled out his wallet. "I need to place an ad."

She angled herself before her keyboard again. "Ready when you are."

"Office help needed. Salary—"

She whipped her head around to look at him in surprise. "I thought Mandy Rogers was working for you."

"She was. She left a couple of days ago for Dallas. Accepted a teaching position there."

Shaking her head with regret, she focused on her computer screen again. "You're going to have a hard time replacing her," she warned. "Not many in San Saba like Mandy. Heart of gold and educated, too."

"Yeah," he agreed glumly. "Red's special, all right. No question about that."

* * *

Mandy sat curled in the corner of the sofa, watching the ten o'clock news with Eddie. Though her gaze was on the screen, her mind was miles away. Specifically, a ranch in San Saba, Texas.

She wondered what Jase was doing, if he'd moved back to his cabin, yet, what he thought of the letter she'd left him. Whether he'd considered contacting his birth parents.

"Eddie?"

"Yeah," he said, his attention focused on the news.

"Do you remember giving Barbara a piece of paper?"

He whipped his head around to look at her. "Yeah. Why?"

"I saw it. Or at least half of it," she amended. "She tore it in two and included one of the pieces in the letter she wrote to Jase, after he was born. Said she wanted each of her children to have something of their father's to keep."

He smiled sadly. "That sounds like something Barbara would have done."

"What was it?" she asked him curiously. "I saw it, but I couldn't make heads or tails out of what was written on it. Other than your name, of course. She tore it in such a way that your first name remained on one piece, your last on the other. Jase got the piece with 'Eddie' written on it."

He turned his face back to the television, but she

could tell he wasn't seeing what was on the screen. His eyes, as well as his mind, were focused on a distant memory.

"It was a bill of sale," he said, remembering. "Or my part of one. A rancher gave a piece of it to me and five of my buddies the day we shipped out for Vietnam. Told us when we got back, we were to join the pieces and bring them to him and he'd give us his ranch."

Mandy's widened in disbelief. "Was he serious?"

He shrugged. "Don't know if he was or not, since we never took him up on his offer. There's a group who's trying to bring all the pieces together now, though. Children of some of the guys. One of them called me awhile back. Name was Vince Donnelly. Preacher's son. I told him I didn't have my piece any longer, but I did pass on Poncho's."

"Preacher and Poncho?" she repeated and laughed.

He smiled, obviously as amused by the names as she was. "Yeah. We all had nicknames. Mine was Fast Eddie." He chuckled softly. "Mine was a joke, 'cause I walked slow even before I lost my foot. Preacher's, though, his fit. You'd never find a man with a kinder heart."

"Why did you have Poncho's piece of paper?"

"Poncho...well, he was a bit of a hellion. That's how he came by the nickname. After Poncho Villa. You know. The leader of the Mexican Revolution. Never understood why he joined the army. Hated rules, and couldn't stand being told what to do.

Finally got a stomach full while we were in Vietnam and took off."

"He deserted?" she asked in surprise.

"I guess you could call it that," he said, then slanted her a look. "He was actually reported as killed in action, but he wasn't. Faked his death, like he died in the battle, then took off for the jungle. Never heard from him again."

"You've got to be kidding! Why would he do a crazy thing like that?"

"Like I said, he hated being in the army. Figured that was his only way out."

"So how did you end up with his piece of paper?"

"He gave it to me the night before he took off. I should've known then he had something up his sleeve, but Poncho was sneaky as hell and could spin a yarn you'd swear was fact. Told me he had a gut feeling he was going to die and wanted me to have his share of the ranch. Even shed a few tears while he fed me that line of bull." Chuckling, he shook his head. "And I believed him. What kind of fool would believe a story like that?"

Mandy grew quiet, her thoughts drifting to the children of the other soldiers and their search for the missing pieces of paper. "And Jase doesn't even know the piece of paper exists."

Eddie glanced her way. "What?"

Not realizing she'd voiced her regret out loud, she shifted uncomfortably on the sofa. "I'm the one who found Barbara's letter," she admitted hesitantly, then decided Eddie had a right to know everything. "Jase refused to read it. Wouldn't even allow me to talk about it."

Eddie turned his face away, but not before she saw the disappointment that softened his eyes.

"He must really hate me," he said miserably.

She dropped to her knees beside his chair and laid a comforting hand on his arm. "How could he when he doesn't even know you?"

"And he won't," Eddie said irritably. "Not as long as he holds this grudge against me."

"I know," Mandy agreed. How could she argue with the truth? Forcing a smile, she gave Eddie's arm a squeeze. "But you never know. He could have a change of heart. Stranger things have happened."

His smile sad, he closed his hand over hers. "You're a sweet girl, Mandy. If nothing else good comes from all this, I've at least had the pleasure of getting to know you."

Eight

After three nights without any rest, Jase gave up on ever being able to sleep again. He didn't even bother climbing into bed any longer, knowing it was a waste of his time. Instead, he watched television and wandered the house. Since he couldn't sleep in his cabin any better than he could in his parents' home, he figured he might as well stay there, where there was at least food prepared for him to eat.

He grimaced at the thought of the food Red had left in the freezer for him. No telling how long it had taken her to cook that much food and store it away. The kindness of the act didn't surprise him. As Suzy

Hopper had claimed at the newspaper office, Red had a heart of gold.

Too bad she had the education Suzy had commended her for, too. If she hadn't, she'd be here with him now, and not in Dallas.

Scowling at the selfish thought, he punched the remote, switching off the TV and stood to stretch. He hesitated a moment, judging his ability to fall asleep, and his scowl deepened, when he deemed himself as wide awake as ever. Heaving a sigh, he strolled barefoot through the house and wound up at the office door.

He paused, telling himself he should at least lie down. He sure as hell couldn't sleep standing up. He snorted a breath, knowing what images awaited him in the bed he'd shared with Red and reached to flip on the light.

He saw it immediately, the bouquet of roses he'd bought for her, and slowly crossed to the desk to pick it up. Still wrapped in the cellophane the florist had placed them in, the wilted roses drooped from their stems. He touched a finger to a petal's dark edge and realized too late that he should have put the roses in water, rather than leave them to die.

Typical, he told himself, and dropped the bouquet in disgust on the corner of the desk. He rarely thought of anything or anyone but himself. He flopped down behind the desk and stared at the neat piles Red had left for him, in an effort to keep his business running smoothly until he could hire a replacement for her. He'd made the first step towards finding a replacement that morning, when he'd placed the ad in the paper.

But how would he ever replace the hole Red's leaving had left in his life? He missed sleeping with her, talking to her, sharing his meals with her. He dragged a hand from the back of his head to the front, making his hair stick up on end. Hell, he just plain missed her. Her laugh. Her smile. The way he'd catch her looking at him, like he was some kind of god or something. He'd always gotten a kick out of her looking at him like that when she was a kid. It had fed an ego that some had claimed was already out of control.

It did nothing for his ego now. The memory only added to the guilt already weighing on him. He'd taken everything Red was willing to give, and what had he given her in return? Groaning, he dropped his elbows to the desktop and his face to his hands, as the answer echoed around his head, pierced his chest.

Nothing. A big fat zero.

She'd never had anything but his best interests at heart. Even when she'd nagged him about finding his birth parents, it was only because she was concerned that he had no family.

He didn't deserve a woman like Red, he told himself miserably. He was nothing but a selfish bastard who'd lived his entire life without a care for anyone or anything. Seeing Suzy Hopper that morning was a perfect example of the self-centered life he'd led. He'd dated the woman for months, yet couldn't even remember her name.

Heaving a sigh, he lifted his head and sank back in the chair. And that's the kind of future he had to look forward to. A constantly changing string of women drifting in and out of his life. Nothing more than one-night stands, really. There might be a sense of safety in relationships like that, but they lacked substance, stability, offering nothing but fleeting pleasure.

Red had provided him with all the things the other women hadn't, plus some. She was a rock to his shifting sand.

And he'd let her slip through his hands.

"She's better off without you," he told himself. She deserved someone with his boots planted firmly on the ground. And how the hell could he ever offer her that kind of life, when he didn't even know who he was, or where he'd come from?

He tensed, realizing he now had the means to answer those questions. Red had all but put the information right in his hands.

He whirled the chair around to face the credenza and yanked open the first file drawer. He flipped past file after file until his gaze rested on "Adoption Papers." Slowly pulling the file from the drawer, he turned the chair back around and opened the file on the desk. Handwritten on a piece of paper clipped to the front cover:

Eddie Davis
2943 Bernhardt Drive
Dallas, TX 75214
Phone: 214-555-6890

He stared at Red's note a long moment, then lifted the letter from his birth mother that lay opposite it. That his hands shook a bit as he unfolded the letter didn't bother him. He figured any man, no matter how strong he considered himself, would be a little nervous at the thought of uncovering his secret past.

He drew in a deep breath and slowly blew it out, before beginning to read.

When he'd finished, he slowly refolded the letter, then turned his gaze to the bookcase to his right and focused his gaze on the framed portrait of his parents that had stood on the middle shelf for as far back as he could remember.

Jason and Katie Calhoun. His parents. He'd loved them from the moment he'd been old enough to recognize the emotion. They were his *parents*, the couple who had loved him and raised him. He turned his gaze back to the letter he held. So who were these people?

He stared a moment longer, than pushed to his feet and grabbed up the file. Tucking it under his arm, he strode out of the office.

It was time he found out.

* * *

Jase parked his truck in front of the house and leaned to study it through the passenger window. He probably should've given the man some warning, he thought, then set his jaw, telling himself the guy didn't deserve the courtesy, considering the lack of consideration he'd given Jase's mother all those years ago.

Snatching up the file, he climbed down from his truck and strode for the door, the chip on his shoulder obvious to anyone who cared to look. He punched the bell once, then tapped his foot impatiently while waiting for a response.

When the door opened, he didn't bother to introduce himself, but went straight to the point of his visit.

"Are you Eddie Davis?" he demanded to know.

The man didn't so much as flinch at Jase's blunt question. He looked him square in the eye and replied, "Yeah, but I think you already know who I am or you wouldn't be here."

Jase held the file up for Eddie to see. "It says in here that you're my father. Is that true?"

Eddie's gaze never wavered from his. "Have you looked in a mirror lately? If you have, I'd think you wouldn't need to ask that question." He stepped back, opening the door wider. "Come on in," he said. "We need to have us a little talk."

Jase hesitated a moment. His anger had brought him this far, but Eddie had quickly stripped him of it by refusing to be intimidated. It was curiosity that made him follow Eddie inside.

As he trailed Eddie down the hall and into the den, Jase couldn't help noticing the man's limp.

Eddie caught him staring and gave his bad leg a pat. "War injury," he said and left it at that.

He gestured to the sofa. "Have a seat. I'm sure you've got questions you want to ask me."

Jase continued to stand. He shouldn't have come here, he told himself. He knew who his parents were. Jason and Katie Calhoun. He didn't need to know any more than that.

"To hell with this," he said, and spun to walk away.

"From what Mandy told me about you, I didn't expect you to be a coward."

Jase stopped short, drew in a furious breath through his nostrils, then turned slowly back around. "If there's a coward in the room, it's *you*. You're the one who walked away from a responsibility. Not me."

Eddie tipped his head to the side to study Jase. "Is that what you think? That I abandoned you?" He shook his head, then waved a hand at the sofa again. "Sit down and hear my side of the story, then you decide if that's what I did."

Jase listened to Eddie talk for over hour, then moved with him to the kitchen when Eddie's throat got dry and sat at the table opposite him, and listened some more, while Eddie alternately sipped water to wet his throat and continued with his tale.

With every fiber of his being, Jase wanted to believe Eddie was lying. That he'd made up the story to make himself appear innocent of any wrongdoing. But Jase couldn't ignore the tears that gleamed in the man's eyes when he talked about Barbara, when he told Jase how much he'd loved her. How the hope of seeing her again was what had carried him through the remainder of the war. How thoughts of her had given him the will to live while he was hiding in the jungle waiting for American troops to return to claim the bodies. How the memory of what he'd shared with her, and hoped to share again with her someday, had given him the strength he needed to get through the surgeries required to repair the damage to his leg and prepare it for the prosthesis he would wear for the rest of his life, and the months of physical therapy that followed the final surgery. How it had taken every bit of nerve he could muster to make the trip to North Carolina to see her, fearing with every mile the bus carried him closer to her that she'd be repulsed by his affliction and want nothing to do with him. How his heart had broken in two when Barbara's mother had told him that Barbara had married. The long years it had taken for the bitterness he felt toward her to fade. How shocked he was to discover that he'd fathered not only a son, but a daughter as well.

Yet, after hearing Eddie's story, he couldn't bring himself to embrace the man, or to even acknowledge him as his father. Eddie might have planted the seed that resulted in Jase's birth, but that didn't make him any less a stranger to Jase.

Eddie smiled sadly. "I know what you're thinking. Nothing I've said has changed anything. I'm still a stranger."

Jase blinked, surprised that Eddie knew his thoughts, then dropped his gaze, ashamed that even after hearing Eddie's side of the story and knowing the hell he had gone through, he didn't feel anything for the man.

Eddie reached across the table and laid his hand over Jase's. "Don't go beating yourself up over this," he said quietly. "I don't blame you for feeling the way you do. The Calhouns raised you. They're your parents. I understand that and respect you for feeling about them the way you do. I'm even grateful to them for raising you into the man you are today." He gave Jase's hand a squeeze. "But I'd like to think I could be your friend. Not your daddy. You've already got one of those. Just your friend."

Emotion rose in Jase's throat and he was afraid for a minute he was going to cry. Eddie might not have raised him, but Jase could honestly say he was proud to know the man responsible for his birth. He rolled his hand over Eddie's to grip it within his. "I'd like that, too."

A smile spread slowly across Eddie's face. "I was hoping you'd say that."

Jase forced his eyes wide to clear the moisture from them and slowly rose. "I've got an errand to run. It may take a while, but I'd like to come back afterwards, if that's okay with you."

Eddie pushed his hands against the table and stood. "That errand wouldn't happen to have anything to do with Mandy, would it?"

Jase looked at him in puzzlement. "Well, yeah. As a matter of fact, it does."

"She's over at the schoolhouse, getting her classroom ready." He glanced at the clock on the kitchen wall, then shot Jase a wink. "If you want to wait, she should be back in another hour."

Stunned, for a moment Jase could only stare. "Mandy's coming here?"

Eddie opened his hands. "Where else would she go? When she left your place, she didn't have a place to stay, and I'm the only person she knows in Dallas."

Jase flipped over the file folder and pulled a pen from his pocket. "Can you tell me how to get there?"

"Sure can," Eddie replied. "Go down to the corner and take a left. Two miles or so down the road you'll see a sign for…"

Jase scribbled as fast as he could, praying that he hadn't destroyed whatever feelings Red had for him when he hadn't asked her to stay.

He added another short prayer that she was as forgiving of his shortcomings as it seemed his birth father was.

Mandy put the finishing touches on the bulletin board she'd decorated, then stepped back to admire her work. "Not bad," she said, with a nod of approval.

"Damn good, if you ask me."

She whirled to find Jase standing in the doorway to her classroom. "Jase." His name slipped past her lips in a stunned whisper.

Smiling, he strode into the room, his hands tucked behind his back and looked around. "Looks like you're ready for the first day of school."

She drew in a slow breath and released it, telling herself his unexpected appearance didn't mean anything. Not what she wanted it to mean, at any rate.

"Getting there," she said. She didn't realize she had used one of Jase's favorite phrases, until she saw him hide a smile. Mad at herself for letting him know he'd had even that small an impact on her life, she crossed to her desk and began shuffling papers. "What brings you to town?" she asked irritably. "A livestock sale?"

"No. Actually I came to see you."

She snapped up her head. "Me?"

His smile widened. "Yep. You." He drew a hand

from behind his back, revealing a very pitiful bouquet of yellow roses. "Sorry they look so bad. I bought them for you the day you left, but you were already gone by the time I got home."

She dropped her gaze at the reminder. "You didn't have to buy me a going away gift," she said quietly.

"Oh, they weren't a going away present."

She glanced up, wondering if she'd made a mistake in leaving, if perhaps the roses were an indication he'd planned to ask her to stay. "They weren't?"

"No." He looked down at the bouquet and plucked at the wilted petals. "Actually I bought them to congratulate you on your new job."

All the hope she'd let build, sagged out of her. "Oh." She forced a smile. "Well, it's the thought that counts."

He cocked his head, a half smile curving his lips. "You know, that's one of the things I love most about you. You can always find a bright spot, even when surrounded by nothing but black clouds."

She rolled her eyes. "Yeah. That's me, all right. Little Miss Mandy Sunshine."

"But there are other things I love even more."

She frowned, wishing he'd quit using the word love. "And what would they be?" she asked tartly.

"Your eyes. Your hair. Your smile. The way you sigh in your sleep. The sound you make after we make love. Half purr, half moan. Sends shivers down my back just thinking about it."

She closed her eyes, letting herself believe for a moment that he meant those things, then opened her eyes to glare at him, knowing he didn't. "What do you want, Jase? As you can see, I've got work to do."

"I can see that," he said, as he moved closer to the desk that stood between them. He held out the bouquet. "These are for you, Red."

She looked at the half-dead roses, sure that this was some kind of joke. But when she looked up at his face, she didn't find a hint of humor in his eyes or his expression. "Well, thanks," she said, and accepted the roses. "I'm sure they were beautiful when they were fresh."

"Not nearly as beautiful as you."

She stamped her foot, having had enough of his teasing. "What are you doing, Jase? Why are you here?"

"I told you. I came to see you. Well, not just you," he amended. "I stopped by to see Eddie first."

Her jaw sagged. "You went to see Eddie?"

At his nod, she pressed her hands over her mouth, to smother a sob. "Oh, Jase. That's wonderful! Did the two of you talk?"

"Actually he did most of the talking. I just listened."

"And—" she prodded, anxious to hear what he thought of his birth father.

"I don't know," he said, suddenly looking uncomfortable. "It's weird, you know? He's my father, yet he's a complete stranger." He dragged a hand down his mouth and shook his head. "We agreed to be friends. Beyond that… I don't know."

Recognizing how difficult it was for him to even accept Eddie on those terms, she quickly rounded the desk and threw her arms around him. "Oh, Jase, I'm so proud of you!" she cried, hugging him tight. "I know how hard it was for you to go and see him." She pushed from his arms and held him by his elbows. "And you shouldn't expect to feel for him what you do for your dad. And I'm sure Eddie doesn't expect you to, either. It's enough that you can be friends."

He smiled and nodded. "Eddie said pretty much the same thing."

When she would have released him, he caught her hands and forced her to remain in front of him. "I had to see him before I could come and see you."

She looked at him curiously. "Why? I didn't hold it against you because you didn't want to meet him."

He tugged her closer and slipped his arms around her waist. "No, you wouldn't do that. You're much too understanding to hold a grudge."

Though there was nowhere she'd rather be than in Jase's arms, Mandy pushed her hands against his chest, trying to break free. "Don't, Jase," she warned. "I can't do this any more."

He tightened his arms around her, refusing to let her go. "Do what?"

Sure that he was purposely trying to drive her crazy, she curled her hands into fists against his chest. "I can't keep on loving you when you don't love me!" she cried angrily.

"Well, that's good."

She dropped her head against his chest, with a groan. "You don't understand. I love you. Really love you. I've been in love with you for as long as I can remember."

"And that's a bad thing?"

Frustrated, she used her fists to push back in his arms. "Yes, it's a bad thing!" she cried. "I can't let myself go on loving you, when you don't love me."

"But I do love you."

"It's insane. Suicidal. It's—" She blinked, as what he'd said slowly registered. "What did you say?"

A smile spread across his face and warmed his eyes. "I love you."

She closed her eyes, gulped, then opened them again. "Say it again."

He dropped his head back and laughed. "I love you, I love you, I love—"

She leaped up to throw her arms around his neck and press her mouth to his.

Cupping his hands beneath her butt, he lifted her higher, and wrapped her legs around his waist, returning her kiss with a fervor that washed away any doubts Mandy might have had that he did truly love her.

"Oh, Jase," she cried softly, burying her face in the curve of his neck. "I didn't know. I swear I didn't know. If I had, I never would've left."

He shifted closer to the desk to sit her down on

its top. "I didn't, either. Or, rather, I *did*. I just was too stubborn to admit it."

She stroked a hand over the face she'd cherished for so many years. "What made you decide you could?"

He caught her hand and brought it to his lips. "Reading the letter my mother wrote. My birth mother," he clarified. "I'd always feared the people responsible for my birth were…I don't know. Bad, I guess. I was afraid I was like them."

"Oh, Jase," she said tearfully. "You're not bad. And they aren't, either. Your mother loved you. That's why she gave you up. She wanted what was best for you, what she felt she couldn't provide herself."

"I know that. Or at least I do after talking to Eddie."

Smiling softly, she combed his hair from his brow. "He's nice, isn't he?"

"Seems to be. Sure doesn't take any crap off anybody. Put me in place fast enough, that's for sure."

Laughing, she hugged him again. "I would've given anything to see that. You two are so much alike, it's scary."

"We are, aren't we?" he said, as if only now realizing that himself. "We even look alike."

"I know," she agreed. "Spooky, isn't it? Looking at him is like looking at an older version of you."

He linked his hands behind her waist. "Think you could live with me, knowing that's how I'll look in another twenty years or so?"

She searched his face, not daring to breathe. "What are you saying?"

Hiding a smile, he reached around her to pick up the bouquet lying on the desk behind her. "If you'd looked a little more closely at your roses, you'd know."

He drew the bouquet around to hold between them. "Check out the ribbon tied around the rose in the center."

With trembling fingers, Mandy separated the roses until she found the ribbon secreted there. A ring was tied within the knot, the diamond at its center caught the overhead light and gleamed. "Oh, Jase," she murmured, recognizing the ring, then lifted her gaze to his. "It's your mother's engagement ring."

He untied the ribbon, freeing the ring, and slipped it over her finger. "And I want you to wear it," he said. "And as soon as we can get you out of this job you were so all fired-up to have, I plan to add the wedding band that goes with it."

She let out a squeal that she was sure could be heard all the way to San Saba, then threw her arms around his neck again. "If that's a proposal, my answer is yes, yes, a thousand times yes!"

Laughing, he scooped her up from the desk and swung her around and around until they were both dizzy, then plopped her down on her feet and caught her hand. "Let's go tell, Eddie," he said, and gave her an impatient tug.

Epilogue

As he had over thirty years before, Eddie stood at the end of the sidewalk, staring up at the house. The house wasn't the same one he'd approached before and definitely had a more prestigious address.

And this time around he wasn't unsure of his welcome.

Knowing he was expected didn't lessen the amount of nerves he currently suffered, but it sure felt good to know that Barbara was waiting somewhere on the other side of the door.

He had to credit Jase with putting him and Barbara in contact again. As it turned out, his son had proved to have a stubborn streak as strong as his old man's. Once he'd located Barbara, he'd started working on locating his twin sister. Eddie had to give Mandy credit for the accomplishment. His new daughter-in-law might not have the stubborn streak he'd passed on to his son, but she had other, gentler ways to get Jase to see things her way.

Even with Barbara's phone number all but shoved into his hand, it had still taken Eddie a while to work up the courage to call her on the phone. His reluctance wasn't due to any resentment he held toward her. He'd dealt with that garbage a long time ago. It was his foot—or rather his lack of one—that bothered him.

Jase had paved the way for him by calling Barbara first. It was actually Mandy's suggestion that Jase should break the ice, so to speak, claiming that Eddie calling might too big a shock for Barbara to withstand. Mandy was right, of course, but then she usually was. She was always thinking of other's feelings and trying to protect them from hurt.

Once Barbara was assured she wouldn't be speaking with a ghost, Eddie had taken the phone. The sound of her voice had knocked him back a good thirty years. They spent that first call crying and apologizing for all that had gone wrong, in spite of the fact that neither one of them were in any way responsible for the things that had happened. More phone calls followed and about a zillion emails exchanged, during which they caught up with each other's lives.

Barbara was a widow now, as her husband had succumbed to cancer three years before. They hadn't had any children together, but her husband had one child, a son, when they married, so she had a stepson to look after her, following her husband's death.

Eddie had less of a life to tell her about. He'd never married, never had any children—other than the twins he'd fathered with Barbara. He'd just worked his whole life, until the company he'd worked for had folded and he had retired.

Dragging himself from his thoughts, he inhaled a deep breath. This is it, he told himself and forced himself to take that first unsteady step up the walk. Aware that she might be watching for him, he squared his shoulders, as he had all those years ago, and concentrated on keeping his gait even to disguise his limp.

He had his good foot on the first step up the porch, when the door swung open and Barbara rushed out. She stopped short and stared, her hands pressed to her mouth, her eyes filled with tears. In spite of the care he'd taken in walking, he was afraid it was his prosthesis that caused her to hesitate. But then she was running, her arms thrown wide, tears streaming down her face.

And Eddie felt as if his feet—both the good one and the prosthesis—were glued to the steps. He couldn't have moved if the devil himself was bearing down on him, planning to drag him off to the bowels of hell.

Barbara flung herself at him and it was all he could do to stand upright, as his bad foot was still on the sidewalk and was forced to bear the brunt of their joined weights.

She hugged him until he was sure she'd squeezed the breath out of him, then drew back to frame his face between her hands. "Eddie. Oh, Eddie," she said tearfully. "I can't believe it's really you."

He gripped her arms, trying not to let on that he was about to topple over backwards. "It's me, all right," he assured her, as he lifted his bad foot to join his good one on the step. Breathing a sigh of relief that he had both legs under him again, he folded his arms around her and held her close.

"What in the world you must think of me," she said and stepped back to sweep the tears from her face. "It's just that I'm so glad to see you," she said, and the tears spilled over her lashes again. Catching his hand, she turned for the house. "Come inside. You must be exhausted from your flight. I promise I won't cry all over you any more. It's just that I'm so excited to see you again and—"

He pulled her to a stop. "Why don't we just get this over with, okay?"

And he kissed her. It wasn't the passionate kiss he'd imagined plastering on her when he saw her again. Those were the dreams of a much younger man, a soldier clinging to a memory to get him through a war he was sure would never end.

But there'd be time for passion, he promised himself, as he drew back to look into the face of the woman he'd never forgotten. He had a lot of fire left in him and years yet to kindle the flame.

Slinging an arm over her shoulders, he urged her toward the door. "I hope you have a beer in your refrigerator. I could sure as hell use one about now."

Laughing, she slipped an arm around his waist and walked with him inside.

* * * * *

Don't miss the conclusion of Peggy Moreland's
A PIECE OF TEXAS,
on sale this January
from Silhouette Desire.

Welcome to cowboy country...

Turn the page for a sneak preview of
TEXAS BABY
by
Kathleen O'Brien
An exciting new title from
Harlequin Superromance for everyone
who loves stories about the West.

Harlequin Superromance—
Where life and love weave together in emotional
and unforgettable ways.

CHAPTER ONE

CHASE TRANSFERRED his gaze to the road and identified a foreign spot on the horizon. A car. Almost half a mile away, where the straight, tree-lined drive met the public road. He could tell it was coming too fast, but judging the speed of a vehicle moving straight toward you was tricky.

It wasn't until it was about two hundred yards away that he realized the driver must be drunk…or crazy. Or both.

The guy was going maybe sixty. On a private drive, out here in ranch country, where kids or horses or tractors or stupid chickens might come darting out any minute, that was criminal. Chase straightened from his comfortable slouch and waved his hands.

"Slow down, you fool," he called out. He took the porch steps quickly and began walking fast down the driveway.

The car veered oddly, from one lane to another, then up onto the slight rise of the thick green spring grass. It just barely missed the fence.

"Slow down, damn it!"

He couldn't see the driver, and he didn't recognize this automobile. It was small and old, and couldn't have cost much even when it was new. It was probably white, but now it needed either a wash or a new paint job or both.

"Damn it, what's wrong with you?"

At the last minute, he had to jump away, because the idiot behind the wheel clearly wasn't going to turn to avoid a collision. He couldn't believe it. The car kept coming, finally slowing a little, but it was too late.

Still going about thirty miles an hour, it slammed into the large, white-brick pillar that marked the front boundaries of the house. The pillar wasn't going to give an inch, so the car had to. The front end folded up like a paper fan.

It seemed to take forever for the car to settle, as if the trauma happened in slow motion, reverberating from the front to the back of the car in ripples of destruction. The front windshield suddenly seemed to ice over with lethal bits of glassy frost. Then the side windows exploded.

The front driver's door wrenched open, as if the car wanted to expel its contents. Metal buckled hideously. Small pieces, like hubcaps and mirrors, skipped and ricocheted insanely across the oystershell driveway.

Finally, everything was still. Into the silence, a plume of steam shot up like a geyser, smelling of rust and heat. Its snake-like hiss almost smothered the low, agonized moan of the driver.

Chase's anger had disappeared. He didn't feel anything but a dull sense of disbelief. Things like this didn't happen in real life. Not in his life. Maybe the sun had actually put him to sleep....

But he was already kneeling beside the car. The driver was a woman. The frosty glass-ice of the windshield was dotted with small flecks of blood. She must have hit it with her head, because just below her hairline a red liquid was seeping out. He touched it. He tried to wipe it away before it reached her eyebrow, though, of course that made no sense at all. Her eyes were shut.

Was she conscious? Did he dare move her? Her dress was covered in glass, and the metal of the car was sticking out lethally in all the wrong places.

Then he remembered, with an intense relief, that every good medical man in the county was here, just behind the house, drinking his champagne. He found his phone and paged Trent.

The woman moaned again.

Alive, then. Thank God for that.

He saw Trent coming toward him, starting out at a lope, but quickly switching to a full run.

"Get Dr. Marchant," Chase called. "Don't bother with 911."

Trent didn't take long to assess the situation. A fraction of a second, and he began pulling out his cell phone and running toward the house.

The yelling seemed to have roused the woman. She opened her eyes. They were blue and clouded with pain and confusion.

"Chase," she said.

His breath stalled. His head pulled back. "What?"

Her only answer was another moan, and he wondered if he had imagined the word. He reached around her and put his arm behind her shoulders. She was tiny. Probably petite by nature, but surely way too thin. He could feel her shoulder blades pushing against her skin, as fragile as the wishbone in a turkey.

She seemed to have passed out, so he put his other arm under her knees and lifted her out. He tried to avoid the jagged metal, but her skirt caught on a piece and the tearing sound seemed to wake her again.

"No," she said. "Please."

"I'm just trying to help," he said. "It's going to be all right."

She seemed profoundly distressed. She wriggled in his arms, and she was so weak, like a broken bird. It made him feel too big and brutish. And intrusive. As if touching her this way, his bare hands against the warm skin behind her knees, were somehow a transgression.

He wished he could be more delicate. But he smelled gasoline, and he knew it wasn't safe to leave her here.

Finally he heard the sound of voices, as guests began to run around the side of the house, alerted by Trent. Dr. Marchant was at the front, racing toward them as if he were forty instead of seventy. Susannah was right behind him, her green dress floating around her trim legs.

"Please," the woman in his arms murmured again. She looked at him, the expression in her blue eyes lost and bewildered. He wondered if she might be on drugs. Hitting her head on the windshield might account for this unfocused, glazed look, but it couldn't explain the crazy driving.

"Please, put me down. Susannah... The wedding..."

Chase's arms tightened instinctively, and he froze

in his tracks. She whimpered, and he realized he might be hurting her. "Say that again?"

"The wedding. I have to stop it."

* * * * *

Be sure to look for TEXAS BABY,
available September 11, 2007,
as well as other fantastic Superromance titles
available in September.

Welcome to Cowboy Country...

TEXAS BABY

by Kathleen O'Brien

#1441

Chase Clayton doesn't know what to think.
A beautiful stranger has just crashed his
engagement party, demanding that he not
marry because she's pregnant with his baby.
But the kicker is—he's never seen her before.

Look for TEXAS BABY and other fantastic
Superromance titles on sale September 2007.

Available wherever books are sold.

REQUEST YOUR FREE BOOKS!

2 FREE NOVELS PLUS 2 FREE GIFTS!

Passionate, Powerful, Provocative!

SDES07

Don't miss the first book in the
BILLIONAIRE HEIRS trilogy

THE KYRIAKOS VIRGIN BRIDE
#1822

BY TESSA RADLEY

Zac Kyriakos was in search of a woman pure both
in body and heart to marry, and he believed that Pandora
Armstrong was the answer to his prayers. When Pandora
discovered that Zac's true reason for marrying her was
because she was a virgin, she wanted an annulment. Little
did she know that Zac was beginning to fall in love with
her and would do anything not to let her go....

On sale September 2007 from Silhouette Desire.

BILLIONAIRE HEIRS:
They are worth a fortune...but can they be tamed?

Also look for
THE APOLLONIDIES MISTRESS SCANDAL
on sale October 2007
THE DESERT BRIDE OF AL SAYED
on sale November 2007

Available wherever books are sold.

COMING NEXT MONTH

#1819 MILLIONAIRE'S WEDDING REVENGE—
Anna DePalo
The Garrisons
This millionaire is determined to lure his ex-love back into his bed. Can she survive his game of seduction?

#1820 SEDUCED BY THE RICH MAN—Maureen Child
Reasons for Revenge
A business arrangement turns into a torrid affair when a mogul bribes a beautiful stranger into posing as his wife.

#1821 THE BILLIONAIRE'S BABY NEGOTIATION—
Day Leclaire
When the woman a billionaire sets out to seduce becomes pregnant, his plan to win control of her ranch isn't the only thing he'll be negotiating.

#1822 THE KYRIAKOS VIRGIN BRIDE—Tessa Radley
Billionaire Heirs
He must marry a virgin. She's the perfect choice. But his new bride's secret unleashes a scandal that rocks more than their marriage bed!

#1823 THE MILLIONAIRE'S MIRACLE—
Cathleen Galitz
She needed her ex-husband's help to fulfill her father's last wish. But will a night with the millionaire produce a miracle?

#1824 FORGOTTEN MARRIAGE—Paula Roe
He'd lost his memory of their time together. How could she welcome back her husband when he'd forgotten their tumultuous marriage?